JUST FIND ME

Carrie Simon

innovo PUBLISHING

Published by
Innovo Publishing, LLC
www.innovopublishing.com
1-888-546-2111

Providing Full-Service Publishing Services for
Christian Authors, Artists & Organizations: Hardbacks, Paperbacks,
eBooks, Audiobooks, Music & Film

JUST FIND ME
Copyright © 2015 Carrie Simon
All rights reserved.

Library of Congress Control Number: 2015939796
ISBN 13: 978-1-61314-273-8

Cover Design & Interior Layout: Innovo Publishing, LLC

Printed in the United States of America
U.S. Printing History

First Edition: August 2015

DEDICATION

To God, above all;

To my children, who never cease to amaze me; and

To my husband, family, friends, and those who bring me inspiration
through extraordinary acts of sincere compassion.

1

Aidan squinted his eyes trying to hold back a string of tears just waiting to fall. His stomach ached, and the palms of his hands and feet had cuts in them from the shards of glass he had been forced to sit on as he was urged to crawl deeper into the old abandoned shed. Initially, it had felt like sharp razors against his skin, but he dared not yell out. No telling what would happen to him if he did. Perhaps if he did everything he was told, maybe, just maybe he would be set free. The wooden boards behind him were wet with a type of green fungus and ivy that had grown all over them, even into the crevices. It made the surface very slimy and gave it a distinctly foul stench, causing Aidan to feel nauseated, as he was forced to inhale the smell for hours. The little light showing through did very little to encourage him, knowing how hard it would be for anyone to find him in such a deserted place. "You had better stay put or it'll be the last thing you ever do!" a gruff voice yelled at him angrily. Aidan tried to use his fingers to tug at the ropes around his wrists and ankles, but it was useless. He grimaced as the ropes dug into his skin, but he didn't flinch. He was still trying to hold back his tears, fearing that his captor would unleash another onslaught of threats of worse . . . carry them out.

"Not scared, are ya? Well you should be, you little snot-nosed brat! Think Mommy and Daddy are gonna come save you? I doubt that very seriously. Once I'm done with you they won't want to find you. And do you know why?"

Aidan didn't say a word, the fear gripping him.

"Ha, because you'll be in pieces, that's why."

Aidan couldn't help it; the tears fell without warning. But his captor was not in the slightest bit moved by emotion. Instead, he grabbed the pocket knife that was attached to his belt and flicked it open. Taking the blade of the knife he scraped at the tears on Aidan's face, reveling in the fear that he instilled in the poor, defenseless child. Suddenly, a sound in the distance startled the captor and he shoved the blade near Aidan's throat, the tip touching his skin ever so slightly.

"I swear I'll kill you right now! No way am I going to let you live and me go to jail. If they plan on catching me, they'll have to kill me to do it," he whispered as he stared into Aidan's eyes.

Aidan stared back and noticed that the eyes of his captor were as black as night, cold, and evil. He had to try to find a way out, seek help, and get home. But how? It had been a couple of days since he had eaten, and his hands and feet felt numb and strange to him as if they were not his. It was going to be a formidable task and not one he was sure his body could endure. What if he was killed trying to leave? On the other hand, something inside of him knew he was dead if he stayed as well. *Better to die trying*, he thought, instantly recalling a phrase his grandfather used to say, having been in the military and served his country proudly.

At first he had been too young to understand his grandfather's words, shrugging them off as the ramblings of an old and weathered man who probably had suffered shell shock in the war. But now he could hear them as plain as day in his ear, whispering to him the message to persevere. Even if the outcome was no good, at the very least he would have tried and given his best effort to get away. However, despite his thoughts, his instant courage soon dissipated only to be replaced with regret. *Why didn't I just listen to Mom?* he thought. *She told me not to go, but I didn't want to listen. That day was just like any other day, riding my bike down the road. Why? Why me?* The more thoughts flooded into Aidan's mind the sadder and more frightened he became. It was almost nightfall again, and there had been no real hope that anyone would find him. He knew in his heart that his parents were looking, but there was no telling where. Everywhere that he had been taken so far was in the woods far away from a television or radio. His pants stuck to his legs, as he had been left with no other choice but to use the bathroom repeatedly on himself. This attracted an array of insects, which he was unable to simply brush away.

His captor was a tall, skinny man with a tan like he had worked outdoors at some point in his life. His eyes were almost pitch-black and sunken. His left cheek bore a small scar near his ear that looked menacing as his leathery face continued to contort into snarls and vicious threats. His faded blue jeans were tattered and torn and hung loosely on his lanky frame. An oversized sweatshirt completed the ensemble that also looked dingy and old as if it had been repeatedly worn without the benefit of a decent wash. A can of chewing tobacco teetered in and out of his left back pocket, which had made an obvious imprint from the time spent there. Every couple of hours he would pull it from his pocket, open it slowly, and grab a finger full of which he would quickly shove down into his mouth and then spit and curse vehemently with no real rhyme or reason for the outbursts. Sometimes Aidan would watch him mumble to himself in words that were unintelligible. And then in other instances, he would sit for a few minutes looking at Aidan, a slow, devilish smile creeping across his face, and let out a fit of giggles before jumping up and pacing around the old shed. Even more alarming was when he would stay sitting and angrily stroke his hair with his dirty hands, later doing the same to Aidan. It was in those moments that Aidan was scared the most. When his captor was so close that his breath would permeate his skin, seeping so deep into him that he thought even a bath could never take the stench off of him.

The closer his captor would get, the further in his mind Aidan would go. His mom had always told him to pray. So, he would close his eyes tightly, squeezing them shut as hard as he could until he could drown out his surroundings, and ask God to help his parents find him. "Please make him stop," he would whisper, though the words never formed on his lips, only in his heart. Not knowing really why, this type of behavior exhibited by Aidan would usually upset his captor and make him do that pacing thing before he would mumble again to himself, cursing under his breath and drinking what was left of the water.

"Bet you're thirsty huh?"

Aidan nodded, snapping back into reality.

"That's too bad; I don't have any for you today . . . maybe tomorrow. If you wake up." He snarled and walked toward a sharp embankment he had affectionately called the "look out." His pocket knife now out and pointed toward an invisible opponent.

Aidan was left alone for the moment, and he felt his body try to relax enough to look around. As a young boy of eleven, he had played many days in the woods such as this, but none of the places he had been forced to hide in looked familiar. *This can't be in Taylor*, he thought, trying to keep his mind on something that may help him escape. The shed was definitely no where he had ever seen before and nothing he had ever recalled any of his friends discussing. He thought about the truck he had been forced into. Green, he thought, trying to focus back on the day. A dark green but he could not recall what kind. It didn't look new and was not the kind his daddy drove. But around Taylor most guys either drove a Ford or a Chevy. And this one hadn't looked like either. Aidan tried to shew a fly away though it didn't do much good seeing as how his hands were tied. He would have to think about the truck some more, maybe he could recall something important, something that might aid him now or perhaps in the future.

***

It had happened so fast, his only reaction was to yell and kick out. A hand had quickly muffled his attempts to call out to his friends and his feeble attempts at kicking also seemed of little difference to his captor. Hadn't somebody looked out of their window? How could a town so small not see anything? It didn't feel like they had driven that far, though the knife poking into his skin had kind of been the only thing he had not forgotten. It had been surreal, as if he was just gonna wake up suddenly and realize he had just been playing one of his video games too long. But it wasn't. The truth of what had happened was instantly and horrifyingly paralyzing. He remembered bragging to his mother as he began to develop some muscles due to his new PE coach.

"Look Mom," he said, proudly lifting his arm up in a ninety-degree angle and flexing his muscle. "Now I dare a bad guy to mess with me." His mother had smiled and Aidan had grabbed her around her waist yelling to his father and younger sisters that he was now strong enough to even lift Mommy up.

"That's good, son, but mommies don't need lifting; they need uplifting, as in tell your mom from time to time how much you appreciate her and what she does for you and your sisters."

"Okay Dad." He shrugged, appearing disappointed. "But I sure would like to try."

"Maybe some other time, Aidan," she said laughing.

***

Aidan looked up trying to push the happy memory away.

"Trying to pretend I don't exist, is that it?"

Aidan was startled. "No, I'm not trying to do anything, I promise. I was just thinking about my mom."

"Oh really?" he sneered, and then leaned his body closer into the dank and dark shed, his breath still smelling of his chewing tobacco. "Well, I tell ya, I don't really care, and what's more important is my knife doesn't either." He patted the side of his pants where Aidan knew the knife hung.

Aidan bowed his head and said nothing, knowing that any comments he made might set his captor off and then no telling what he'd do. His behavior of compliance had worked so far, but he knew that it was about to be exhausted, and a plan to escape would have to be formulated in order to survive. The sun had set and not much had been accomplished as far as his recollections of what had transpired. He could feel eyes staring at him as the day soon drifted into night, and again he closed his eyes in prayer. "Please God. Please don't let him touch me," Aidan prayed.

"What was that? You said something?" his captor asked.

Aidan sat quietly hoping that he would presume he was sleeping, but it was no good.

"I know it's you." He inched closer and Aidan felt a shiver run down his spine. "And I know you are awake, so ready or not . . . HERE I AM!"

Aidan screamed loudly when he finally saw the whites of his captor's terrifying eyes glowing in the dark.

"Oh you're gonna get it now, boy," he said, grasping out in the dark making contact with Aidan's head.

The next few moments felt like they were in slow motion. Aidan tried to brace himself for the blow, thinking this was finally it, but instead his captor lunged at him without his knife, choosing to thrust his fist into Aidan's temple instead. Aidan felt himself falling over on some more pieces of glass, but there was nothing he could do to stop it or prevent the pain he knew he was about to feel. He was helpless. He fell with a thud and lost consciousness. His captor, feeling frustrated, left the shed not yet ready to finish what he had started, though the idea did cross his mind. But all that noise might have riled someone up, and he needed to get to his lookout just in case someone had heard the noise. He would have to finish off anyone who may have come out looking.

Aidan awoke abruptly to something creepy coming toward his mouth and achingly spit at it realizing he was still alive. The small bug fluttered for a moment then flew away as Aidan tried to open both of his eyes a little further. The right side of his head ached painfully and his face felt swollen, but he still had his wits about him. He scanned around the shed for his captor, but he was nowhere to be seen. *Probably at the lookout again*, Aidan thought. He tried to put his body in a kind of contortionist twist to try to be able to lift himself up and back in a sitting position. It was more difficult than he originally thought. The feces and urine inside of his pants had dried making his pants stiff and hard to adjust. He began to wiggle his toes and fingers a bit making sure that they were still there so he could possibly use them to shift himself around and hopefully, with enough momentum, turn onto his back and then up again. He began to move ever so slightly in order to avoid more cuts from the glass that he knew lay underneath him. After successfully positioning himself onto his back with a bit of effort he was able to once again be in an upright position and assess his surroundings. His head felt wobbly and he seemed dazed as he tried to focus his eyes on an object in the old shed.

Everything seemed blurry now that he was sitting up. Maybe he wasn't okay, he thought objectively. Aidan tried to recall the events just before he blacked out. He knew his scream had upset his captor, but the scream had been totally involuntary. He hadn't meant to, just everything was so frightening and then the dark came, absolute blackness. *Wait*, he thought, there was something else in his eyes. Aidan recalled staring at him right before . . . nothingness. Soon he would be back again as he always would, but with the passing of each and every day it became more and more urgent for him to get away. With the beginnings of sunlight for a new day and another moment to himself, Aidan needed to keep thinking of something that might abet him in his escape. But what? Not much in the dilapidated shed for that matter was of any worth. The whole place was old, worn down, and deteriorating quickly. The objects that hung on the wooden walls by metal hooks had long been rusted as was the hooks themselves. Besides, everything was too high for any normal child to reach, much less one whose hands and feet were already bound.

A few tattered ropes lay in another corner adjacent from Aidan, and beer bottles lay scattered about that had not been broken like the ones that lay in shards all about him. At first he had imagined using one of the pieces like he had seen in a spy movie to cut at the ropes his wrists were bound with. But his captor was constantly checking on him so if he were caught trying to cut at the ropes, he knew it was death for sure. If he were somehow able to get the ropes from off his wrists, the chances of him getting them off his ankles in time were doubtful. This had to be perfect if it was going to work, and then because he was not really sure where his parents or the police were, he would have to hide and lay low. He needed access to some water since he was already feeling weak. If he disobeyed again, though, he may go another day without water and then be too tired to even make the escape. Aidan closed his eyes again, squinting away the tears that had formed on the sides of his face and hoping they would fall and dry before his captor returned. The undertaking of survival seemed nearly impossible, and the hopes of being found alive felt further and further away from reality. He tried to envision his mother and father along with his two younger sisters frantically looking for him. He hoped to use his mind to call out to them, wishing that some sort of telepathic signal would reach them in time. But that was silly and he dispelled the thought. *Pray*, he thought. He could continue to pray. It had worked thus far.

Maybe Mom was right; maybe prayer really did have power, the supernatural kind. He had attended Sunday school ever since he could remember. All of the characters they would study about seemed to have that in common. They all would pray. Aidan wasn't sure that all that stuff actually happened, but he knew Mom and Dad said it did . . . all of it. He remembered his Sunday school teacher telling him a story about a Bible character named Daniel. He was taken away into another country. *That's kinda like kidnapping*, he thought. Focusing on the story he tried to wiggle his wrists and feet around. It was useless. The ropes were so tight that the only thing it did was cut further into his skin, and he yelped. "Ugh," he said, trying not to speak too loudly. Voices from behind the shed caused him to try to turn his head in that direction, but he could not see anything. He knew it was his captor, but what he was doing was only a guess.

"Bet you're wondering what I'm up to, huh?" his captor said, coming toward Aidan a few minutes later as if he had read Aidan's mind. "I got me a few booby traps so that nobody is gonna make their way here without paying for it. It's almost done; did most of it while you were still lying in your spit. Ha!"

Aidan stared through the open doorway and into the woods, his eyes scanning the perimeter for anything that looked different. This new development was going to hurt him as much as somebody else. If he were to get loose and then wind up caught in one of his so-called traps, it was gonna be a bad ending as well. He decided perhaps a different approach might coax his captor into revealing more information.

"So," Aidan's voice stammered as he tried to speak with confidence, "you have a bunch of traps?"

His captor seemed a bit surprised at his boldness but spoke after a few minutes as if he had been lost in his thoughts moments prior. "Yeah, I got a few," he said proudly. He paused and then spoke again. "Some fairly decent and others that I just might have to pat myself on the back for." He chuckled and stared at Aidan. "Why, what's it to you?" His dark eyes now boring into Aidan's. "I know you ain't thinking of no hare-brained ideas about trying to leave this place without me. Cuz if you do, I got one that'll have you hanging like a scarecrow."

Aidan shuddered, his whole body suddenly cold. "I wasn't thinking that," he said.

"Yeah right, I'm not stupid! I see you looking around. But that's why I brought you here. Cuz there ain't nothing for you except me. I say if you eat, if you drink . . . I am and will be the *last* face you will ever see."

Aidan wanted to cry, but he knew that if he was going to make it he would need to toughen up. "But aren't you worried you're gonna forget where all those traps are?" Aidan interjected, pretending to switch the conversation and act unperturbed by his captor's last comments.

"Do you know who you are talking to? You're talking to one of the best. Why, I flat out idolize myself sometimes."

"Like now?" Aidan asked, trying to force the conversation to last longer.

"I doubt anyone ever used the kinda tricks I use. Like them there trees for instance, once them stupid cops come scurrying up here, those trees are gonna snatch them up and have 'em hanging by their toes," he said.

"So it's just tree traps?" Aidan questioned, raising his eyebrows.

"No, you little brat, I got me traps all around this shed too. But . . ." he said, pausing to let out a maniacal laugh, "those I can't tell you about."

Aidan tried to move around a little since his hands were feeling numb again. "I'm thirsty; can I have a little water?"

"Humph, from the smell of your pants, I'd say you had too much to drink already."

"Please I didn't have any yesterday, and I really need some bad. I can hardly swallow. Please, just a little?" Aidan begged sincerely. He watched as his captor mulled over the idea. At first, Aidan thought he may slap at him for asking or worse refuse to give him any for another day, which might make him unable to ever bother fighting to break free. But after a brief silence, his captor picked up the small container of water and eased the opening to Aidan's lips.

"Better not drink it all," he said.

Aidan gulped hungrily, the water slowly running into his mouth and cooling his throat. Before he could get another, however, his captor pulled it quickly and cruelly away from his lips.

"Can't be having all that now, you might get spoiled," he told him.

Aidan licked at his lips grateful for every drop. How he wished he could have just a few more sips and maybe a bite to eat, but it wasn't worth it. He would keep his mouth shut and maybe he would be given some more water later.

His head still ached, and he wondered if he had a knot on his head from either being hit or from the ground where he had landed. There was no way to tell because he could not free his hands to touch anything. For now he had to just survive. Everything else he had been dealing with in his life, like school, friends, skateboarding, sports . . . all seemed so insignificant compared to all that was happening. He tried to imagine his friends reading about him in the paper and the desk at school empty without him in it. He could even visualize a few of their faces. They all seemed to be staring back at him as if he were a specter. *They probably think I'm dead*, he thought. Aidan tried not to let himself give up, but it was becoming difficult not to lose hope. With no real chance of making it, his heart began to feel discouraged and he continued to stare at the wooden slabs pretending they were people all telling him good-bye.

"What are you staring at? You look like you're seeing things." His captor angrily slapped the back of Aidan's head and almost toppled him over.

"I was just looking," Aidan said, trying once again to draw a little more information from him.

"Looking at what? The only thing you need to be doing is thinking about what I'm gonna do to you if you even as so much make a sound that I don't like. Course you wouldn't, huh?" he asked sarcastically. "You got knocked out and all last night. Wouldn't want my anger to be getting the better of me now would we? Then I might wind up cutting you up into pieces like I did that kid from Green Valley. Boy, now that was a handful."

Aidan shuddered again, hoping that he was just telling him that to make him scared. But he wasn't too sure. Seemed like something he had heard before. Like it sounded familiar to him and it made him suddenly want to vomit.

"Why, why would you do something like that, Mister?" Aidan replied quietly as he struggled with the realization of his own similar fate.

"I didn't do anything . . . at least as far as you are concerned." His captor turned and walked up to him and bent over to stare at him squarely in his eyes. "See, the first thing you got wrong is thinking that any of this conversation here matters at all to me. Second, I like boys, always have. The law don't want me to be myself so I can't have you running your mouth off after our little time together. Once I get what I want, I don't need you anymore. So, there it is . . . like it or not." Aidan began to cry. Not a few tears, but really weep. "Oh no, you're not gonna start that crap around me again. I'll gut you right now!" Aidan's lips quivered and he did his best to stop. "Now . . . that's better," his captor said, kissing him on the cheek. "It's best to just let it happen."

Aidan closed his eyes praying, *Please God, please help them find me!* He looked upward and something caught his eye. It was a small hay loft almost completely hidden by the fungi and ivy that had grown all around it. In fact, Aidan had originally thought that the wood had rotted there and the ivy had just simply taken over the area. But he was wrong. It was definitely a small loft that appeared intact and just enough for someone small to hide. Suddenly, a plan came to mind. Once it got dark, he would have to try. This was it and his mind raced with thoughts of how to pull off such a harrowing and formidable escape.

2

Roy Brown looked like nothing more than the average drifter making his way through town after town. His sandy brown hair and dark eyes didn't make him stand out all that much. He was tall and lanky with a medium build and a nice smile. Jeans and tennis shoes typically completed his usual look, which was so common that nobody ever raised an eyebrow. As an outsider he was given the up and down glance fairly standard to drifters, but that was about it. He might have looked in financial straits but definitely not menacing. A look he felt proud he could perform convincingly and eventually get lost in the crowd, becoming just another person in the sea of random people. He had grown up in a small Southern town in North Carolina, brought up by a single mom who enjoyed getting high more than being a mom. She would tell him every once in a while that his daddy had left them when he was young, only to hear her later telling other neighbors that she never knew who his father was. So Roy began to not even bother to ask her about his father, knowing that he no doubt would be given whatever story she decided to concoct for the day. In fact, not long after the realization that his mother was a drug addict and liar, he began running away each day after school to anybody who would take him in. Day after day, his hatred for not only his mother but for all women grew until he could hardly stomach their presence. By the age of eleven or twelve, he had already managed to get picked up for shoplifting, and at fifteen he'd spent a couple of weeks in "juvie," though no one seemed to care.

His mother had never opted to visit, and he wasn't upset by it. He hated her. For a couple of years after dropping out of school he had made a few attempts to try to figure out who his father might be, but it was useless. His mother was never able to provide much information, and when he did go visit her it would send him into a spiral of anxiety, depression, and hostility. He had tried a few jobs here and there to make ends meet, but he'd never stayed too long. He didn't like having anyone boss him around, and on a couple of the jobs he'd even been run off after threatening a couple of coworkers.

Finally, it occurred to him that he might have better luck if he moved away. But he didn't have much money. The only one who had anything was his mother and that was only because she had inherited the home she lived in from her parents after they passed away. Pretty much everything else of value had been squandered or pawned to keep her drug habit satisfied. Only sparse, unmatched furniture littered the house, all of it cheap and old. *Gotta get out of here*, he thought. He recalled the night he had gone to see his mother to ask about the house. She was sprawled on her tattered recliner with the drugs sitting on her lap. He had knocked a couple of times but realizing the door was open, walked in.

She appeared almost in a trance as he tried to shake her by her shoulders. She turned her head to him to speak, but her words were almost inaudible and her glassy eyes stared out as if she were looking through him. He couldn't stand it any longer and began to pace around as he waited for her to sober up enough to speak to him plainly. And then it happened—the onslaught of sinister thoughts crept into his head and wormed and shaped its way into what he thought was a brilliant idea. "It would be so simple," he said aloud to himself and reached for the drugs.

His mother, still dazed, opened her mouth to speak. "R-O-Y, is that you?"

"Uh, yes. Sure is."

"R-O-Y, what are you doing here?" she asked, still slurring badly.

"Oh nothin', Momma, just came here to visit ya and see how you were doing."

"R-e-a-l-l-y? Why you bein' so nice? What . . . you . . . really . . . came . . . here . . . for?"

Roy recalled not saying a word as he slowly picked up the bag of drugs and emptied it all into a small glass of water. The contents began to fizzle a bit as he swirled the small glass around to stir the contents.

"I know you're probably thirsty, Momma. Let me just get you something to drink. Something you're gonna like." Roy put the glass to her lips and began to pour the contents down her throat. She choked for a moment and then relaxed, finally giving up any resistance to his strange behavior. A few more drinks followed, but this time with the contents from her medicine cabinet. Roy continued to watch her as she drifted further and further away from reality. Her body convulsed a few hours later and then nothing. Finally, it was over. He had done it and now he could sell the house and get out of that filthy place. His plan seemed flawless, and he giggled to himself as he called 9-1-1.

He stood in front of a mirror in the living room as he spoke into the receiver, pretending to be auditioning for a role on television. "Hello?" he said frantically, "please help my mom; she's not breathing."

"Yes, sir, please stay on the line while we send someone to that location. Can you verify the home address?" the dispatcher asked.

"Yes, it's 925 Oak Drive. Please come quickly. I just got home and found her like this. Oh my goodness, I can't believe this is happening! I hope she's not dead!" Roy tried to sound scared but inwardly he did everything he could not to burst into fits of laughter.

"Okay, sir, it's going to be okay. What is your mom's name?"

Roy looked again at himself in the mirror and smiled, while still answering her questions. *Yes, it is gonna be okay,* he thought. *Soon everything will be mine and I'll be long gone.*

He continued to stare at himself and applaud his own performance as the patrol car showed up along with the ambulance. The medics were the first to run in, and they began administering first aid. But after multiple attempts, they moved her to the ambulance to continue their lifesaving efforts. However, Roy knew it was too late for his mother. A new chapter of his life was about to begin, and the only thing left for him to do now was go through the process of burying her and collecting the proceeds.

"Sir, can you tell me just what happened?" an officer asked while walking toward Roy and then stopping in the door way. Perhaps they were surprised that he did not immediately rush toward the ambulance, but then again, maybe not. He knew he needed to play it cool and stay calm if this scheme of his was going to work. His mother had already had a few run-ins with the law and no doubt didn't leave a good impression in their minds.

"Well, I was just going off in to town, you know, and I came back home to see my mom and that's how I found her," he said to the officer, his voice beginning to shake though not from sadness but out of apprehension.

"Can you give me an approximate time you arrived?" the officer asked as he took out a small notebook and began writing in it.

"I dunno, right before I called you guys. Couldn't have been more than a couple of minutes prior. I mean, I walked into the living room you know, like this . . ." He began motioning with his hands as if he were demonstrating how he had just walked in and discovered her. "Like I said, that's when I saw her."

"Okay, and what did you do next?" the officer asked, looking up from his notebook.

Roy put his head down letting it linger for a moment. "Then I came to her, you know, tried to see if she was still breathing, and she wasn't. I don't know all that CPR reviving stuff, so I just called 9-1-1 and that's about it."

Roy tried to think of something sad to make him cry, but the only thing that come to mind was having to sit on death row. The officer continued to write as Roy kept his head down hoping that it would not be too obvious that his eyes were dry. Try as he might, Roy just could not make the tears appear. *Cry, dang it!* he thought, cursing mentally at himself. The officer continued to write and to look around at some of the items in the house including the recliner that his mother had been found on. *First thing I'm gonna do when this is over is set that stupid chair on fire,* Roy thought as he quickly tried to hide the smile that was growing despite their presence.

"We still have to get some more information from you, sir, but we are just going to give you a call tomorrow. In the meantime, we understand that you are probably anxious to get to the hospital to be with your mom."

"Uh, oh yes . . . yes, sir," Roy said, looking up. He fumbled to get his hands out of his pockets and retrieve his keys from the metal hanger beside the door. He felt like the officer was now staring at him, and it was starting to get on his nerves. He needed to get outta there and the recent comments now gave him an excuse to do so. With the knowledge that he needed to simply play along, Roy let the officer follow him out of the house and toward his truck.

"I'm sorry for your mother, son, hope she pulls through," he interjected and got into his patrol car.

Roy waved bye and climbed into his truck, rolling down the window and spitting as he spoke to himself. "Well, for one I ain't your son, and two, I hope she's dead." He drove off, once again feeling elated at the new developments.

For the next seventy-two hours, he continued to be subjected to a litany of questions and sympathies, both of which almost led him to madness or confession. But he'd held out, making pleasantries, finalizing the sale of the home. All in all it had taken him another eight months to finally gather the funds he needed to pack up and get out of that town. The sale of the house had been less than what he'd eventually hoped for, but the truth was that it had not been kept up during his mother's lifetime and he was not about to put money into the property himself. "As is" was his echo as the paperwork was signed.

He had a few debts that he had incurred, and though he debated whether or not to skedaddle and leave the bill collectors hanging, he decided to go ahead and square up with them. He was ready for a fresh start and knew the last thing he needed was for them to find out his whereabouts and start pestering him again. This left even less in his hands but with the emptying out of the account, a large sack of clothes, and a few other odds and ends, he was set. His old, beat-up Toyota had been paid off and was still running. *Time to kiss the town good-bye*, he thought smugly as he filled up one last time at one of the local gas stations. He'd even purchased a map of the United States and decided he might like to just sightsee for a while. It wasn't like there was anything or anyone to hold him back now. So, he began to simply drive, sometimes sleeping at the various state rest areas, and other times just hunkering down in his truck in a truck stop that didn't seem too busy. Unhurriedly going through the scenic routes a few times, he would stop and get out, looking around at all the families having picnics or playing outside with a pet or two.

How pathetic, he thought, driving off. He didn't need mushy garbage like that. Sooner or later he would find a place that he liked enough to stay and then he'd be able to just settle down and pursue other things he had in mind. Funds had continued to dwindle though he had managed to use it sparingly. But still, with gas and food, he didn't want to run the risk of getting somewhere and having to panhandle. Besides, the truck wasn't in the best shape, and he definitely didn't want his funds being depleted on repairs. Sooner or later he'd have to maybe catch a job or two to replenish his stash and money.

A few days later he had passed through Georgia and into Alabama. The weather, without air conditioning in his truck, was almost unbearable. But he pressed on. He knew no one had pieced together his mother's murder, but he still felt the need to get as far away as he could. With a little bit of work, he could become just another country boy driving a truck and out to make a living. These people didn't know a thing about him or his past and he liked it like that. He could literally be anyone he wanted. Looking at himself in the rearview mirror he studied the face staring back at him. "Roy, you sly fox, time to become whoever you want." He smiled a toothy smile and rubbed his fingers through his hair as the wind continued to blow it back and forth.

He was pretty sure that a few newspapers somewhere would probably provide him with some income. So now to just pick the town. He was looking for somewhere not too big, not too small, and where he might explore a few of his fantasies. Ever since he was in his teenage years, girls had disgusted him, not just some girls, all girls. *Disgusted isn't even the right word*, he thought. *Repulsed is more like it.* Every time they would look at him batting their eyes, he saw his mother and her lies and it would make him ill for days. Boys were more his thing, not too young but not too old to question his authority. His hometown had been too small to explore any of his desires since he had grown up with many people there. But away now he was free to do whatever he wanted. He closed his eyes for a moment and then looked up—a sign on the right side of the highway stated a town was about five miles away. Roy bit his lip and repeated the name aloud—Green Valley. It sounded perfect and he said it again, this time slower and forceful. He finally veered toward the appropriate exit and combed his fingers through his hair again with anticipation.

Green Valley was just as he expected. Like most Southern towns, everything in the town was built around the square or central location that usually held a courthouse, public offices, and local shops. Roy knew if he drove down the main road in town he was sure to run right into the center of it. Before long, there stood the town square and right in the center a looming building with Green Valley Courthouse on its façade. It was massive and by the looks of it had been erected quite some time ago. Roy smiled to himself, parked his truck, and rolled his window down. The weather was unpleasantly warm and humid, but he stuck his arm out anyway, letting it move in the air as if he were running his fingers through strands of air.

He felt comfortable here and decided he would grab a few groceries to eat and buy a few local papers. It hadn't been too difficult and with very little effort he had collected both and was parked in a

23

supermarket parking lot. He was far enough away to not be bothered and yet close enough to still have the overhead lights in order to read the classifieds.

Roy studied the papers for a few minutes before putting down some of the articles and perusing the help-wanted ads. He wanted to take a good look at the people, get a feel for this town, and familiarize himself so that he didn't feel eyes on him everywhere he'd go. *Need to make these people trust me*, he thought. *Need to see how I can connect with them, get them to relax, and welcome me in.* He laughed at that notion. Something about them unknowingly welcoming in a murderer seemed so amusing.

Roy put down the papers with the faces of the townsfolk plastered on each and every page. They all looked so seemingly happy. Why wasn't he? Didn't he deserve to be happy? Roy shook his head as if fighting something undetectable to the human eye and picked up the classifieds.

A few listings offered temporary work, and Roy decided they were worth the phone call. He knew one of the jobs he might have a little difficulty getting, being that he didn't have much experience, but the other he could easily do and he was pretty sure it wouldn't require a thorough search of his background either. So, he decided to call. He drove his truck to the front of the store, parked, and walked up to the phone booth to dial the number.

"Lynn's Restaurant, Tony speaking."

"Hello, Mr. Tony." Roy's voice was even and calm. "I was calling about the ad in the paper for a dishwasher. I wasn't sure if the position was filled, and if it isn't then I'd like to apply for the job." Roy bit into his lip nervously, almost drawing blood. He really hated socializing with people, but he knew that he would have to keep his cool and be polite for now.

A long pause ensued, followed by a few questions to which Roy answered, his voice unwavering, "Yes," he was available tomorrow. "Yes," he had reliable transportation. "No," he wouldn't have a problem submitting to a drug test. "Yes," he had a nice shirt and slacks.

Roy was just about to get tired of the questions, but then he was given a time to show up. He would begin tomorrow at 5:00 p.m.

No excuses. He hung up the phone and walked to his truck. He knew he needed a shower and decided that tonight's achievements warranted a hot one with a nice clean bed. He would find a cheap hotel. The town actually had a few motels and hotels to choose from. In fact, there were five to be exact. Most of them looked pretty crowded and since it was a little bit of a splurge, Roy didn't want to get carried away with it. One of the smaller hotels offered a rate that he liked, and breakfast was part of the deal. He drove down the little frontage road and into the parking lot. A few cars were parked, but besides that it was quiet.

Roy parked and opened up a small duffel bag, pulling a crisp hundred dollar bill out and zipping the duffel bag closed again. He then walked to the front of the hotel and rang a small silver bell that sat all by itself on the counter. A middle-aged man of Middle-Eastern decent came walking to the front to greet him. Within a few minutes, he was inside his room and relaxing as he looked through the channels on the television set. Much of it was sports, but Roy found a local station that was airing a news segment and decided to leave it there.

A "big to do" was for the Green Valley Bobcats—a local baseball team for boys ten to twelve. Roy bit his lip again and continued to stare at the footage of their latest victory over a rival team. He tried not to think too much about it, chiding himself for even looking at such a thing knowing how he felt.

"Mustn't think about all that right now," he said aloud to himself. He knew he had a job now in a brand-new place, and he needed to be presentable.

Straightening his back, he got out of the bed and into the bathroom to take a shower. The water smelled a little funny, but it was hot and felt good. It cascaded over him and instantly relaxed his tired muscles. "See, Mother, I did amount to something . . . oh wait…you aren't here to see it. Ha ha ha!" Roy's laugh became louder and louder.

"Hey, knock that off!" someone said, banging against the wall.

He quickly quieted himself and exited the shower for fear that the night clerk would be called. But he didn't hear anymore sounds and soon fell asleep in bed clutching the small duffel bag.

Morning came early as the sun's rays trickled in through the curtains. At first he thought about simply putting the blankets over his eyes and drifting back to sleep but ultimately decided against it. He needed to be awake and get a head start to see where he needed to be for work. Although he had a physical address for the restaurant, he thought it better to explore, see where the restaurant was, and maybe have lunch in one of the local eateries. A map on the back of a hotel brochure provided a rather crude but legible street guide, complete with a listing of local events, shops, restaurants, and main attractions. One of those listed was Lynn's Restaurant.

Not too far from here, he thought. "Heck, I could almost walk there and back before checkout." Roy picked up his jeans and shirt from the day before and put them back on. Before long he was strolling down the sidewalk and whistling a song he had heard on the radio while driving. He had originally thought about putting his duffel bag in the security box in the room but opted to put it back in the truck. He had read once that those safes were bogus and he didn't want to chance it.

The stroll to the restaurant wasn't too long, but the weather had already started to change and Roy could feel the raindrops randomly falling and landing on his shoulders and face as he walked. Picking up the pace, he arrived shortly thereafter at his new employment. The place was deserted. The hours stated they only opened in the evenings, but this was perfect. Roy didn't like the idea of working too much anyway. He really didn't need that much for the few necessities he required, such as lodging, food, and gas. He had slept many times in his truck and eaten beans from a can, so as long as he could afford to lay low and stay in the hotel for a while, he was perfectly satisfied. The raindrops started to fall faster and with more force, causing Roy to look up at the darkening sky and curse at it. *So much for the sightseeing tour.* He turned on his heels, making good time back to the hotel.

Although it took him less time to return to the hotel, he was drenched when he arrived. The day clerk said nothing as he strolled right through the small lobby and into a room where he could see piping hot biscuits, fluffy eggs, and a variety of muffins. He poured himself a cup of coffee and sat down at one of the small tables. A couple who had been sitting nearby quickly left, leaving him to leisurely eat and smile sardonically, "Didn't like you either," he said to himself, recalling the look in their eyes as he left a puddle of water near the coffee carafe. He glanced up to see that the time to check-out was quickly approaching. He had enough time for a shower but decided that he could afford another night. "Might as well," he reasoned to himself. "I want to make a good impression on my first day of work."

Minutes later, he lay once again on the hotel bed, dry and flipping through the channels again. He had a few hours to waste. An old black-and-white movie caught his attention, and he made himself comfortable by propping up his pillows and stretching his legs out. Before too long, he had drifted to sleep. Suddenly, the alarm by his bed began to beep loudly. Roy jumped up and slapped at the clock, turning off the alarm. *Good thing I set that.* He quickly dressed and glanced at himself one last time in the mirror before he headed out to the restaurant.

3

Luke and Linda Williams had moved to Taylor back in the 80s and had never wanted to move elsewhere. The parks, schools, and friendly atmosphere had made it the perfect choice for them. They had been ready to start a family and felt comfortable to do so. At first, with his career in pharmaceutical sales and her an interior designer, the dream of being able to put off the careers and have children had been just that, a dream. And then there it was—the two-story gabled home, the sound of children, the decision to have a one-income household. Aidan was the first. Linda reminisced about the day she had called Luke at his office.

"Hon, I'm in a conference right now can I call you later?" Luke tried to sound like he wasn't in too much of a hurry.

"Sure," she said, placing her mouth close to the receiver "It can wait." Although she had hoped to simply blurt out the good news, she realized she'd have to wait to tell him later. The hours seemed like an eternity before he called her back.

"Okay, hon, I'm done. Didn't mean to put you off, just this conference meeting was a big one and I was right in the middle of it. Please accept my apology, I'm sorry."

Linda had always appreciated Luke's thoughtfulness. Although she knew he did not always understand her moods or behavior, he had faithfully made it a point to be mindful of her needs and desires.

"Sweetie, no need for an apology. I called you at work and I know that you being busy is what is to be expected. But now that you are on your way, I'm simply gonna wait and tell you when you get home."

"Is it something bad? Are you okay?" Luke's voice worried.

"No, no, nothing like that. Everything is fine; it can wait now until you get home."

Luke pulled in the driveway halfway thinking that there was still something amiss, but his wife's voice had been calm, almost reassuring, so he stepped out of the vehicle and hit the button for the garage door to close. Linda was there, smiling from ear to ear with a small box in her hands. Luke instantly knew the cause for her delight. She was pregnant and he grabbed her up in his arms, swinging her around and then down to the ground, kissing her fully on the lips.

"How'd you guess?" she said, looking up at him lovingly.

"Oh, I dunno. Guess I haven't seen a grin like that since you walked down the aisle and we looked at one another." He laughed as he spoke and pushed the loose strands away from her face.

"I'm sure there were a few other times," she said, softly punching his shoulder playfully.

He smiled back at her. She was beautiful with long, brown hair and doe-like eyes that sparkled when she was happy. He knew she had always loved children and now would make an excellent mother. Of that, he had no doubt.

The days of that first bliss and anticipation soon turned to months, and before a new year had begun, they had welcomed their very first child. Linda had wanted to choose the name, and he did not deny her request. She seemed so eager that it almost was without question.

"His name is Aidan!" she said as they brought him into the hospital room with his little receiving blanket warmly covering him and surrounding his small body like a cocoon. He was so delicate and small that they both stared for hours at such a wondrous gift. It had almost felt surreal but soon the days would be full of hectic schedules, diapers, cries in the night, and child proofing the entire house. But somehow despite the upcoming adjustments, none of it seemed to damper the happiness that they both had felt that day.

Soon, Aidan was growing from a small infant into a precocious toddler and then into an intelligent boy full of wonder, curiosity, and courage. Nothing seemed too impossible to him in his eyes. His mother and father also welcomed two new additions to their lives, twin daughters, Riley and Raney, five years later. Luke had gotten a promotion at the pharmaceutical company and both had decided that Laura was needed more at home raising the little ones. Truth be known, she had grown tired of feeling obligated to pursue her career. She had initially been a very sought-out interior designer, but the days of feeling that its accolades were enough were over. She gladly preferred the kiss of her children rather than the vain praise of strangers who not only did not really know her but had chided her decisions through the years as a slap in the face of feminism. If they only knew how much things had improved since they decided to raise a family and her take a break from her career. She had often thought of all the laughs, tears, and firsts she had experienced that would not have been afforded to her had she not made her choice.

"Darlin', what was going through your mind?" She could hear her so-called colleagues echoing their disapprovals. "I mean you were good, real good. Now, it's like you're some Rapunzel locked up in that house, forced to take care of kids, and be subjected to only Disney movies."

They had all cackled, but Linda and Luke were never happier. Their children were good kids, students, and into a few sports during the summer months. Taylor wasn't that large of a town, but the population of twenty thousand still provided plenty of diversity and yet a warm, friendly neighborly feel to the entire town. They had been so pleased that they had always felt welcome in such a nice town without having grown up there. Even the church they attended had always been so thoughtful. Aidan had made many friends there and so did the girls who attended gymnastics along with many of their schoolmates. Life seemed to be going along splendidly until that day. As usual, Luke was headed back from work and had phoned Linda to ask her if she needed him to pick something up for dinner.

"No, hon," she had replied, "I've already started dinner. Aidan had football practice today and rode his bike to the field. He should be arriving about the same time as you."

Aidan had started pee-wee football when he had been very young and had recently made the cut for Taylor Middle School. He was versatile and extremely athletic, and his coach had played him as both wide receiver and quarterback. Much to everyone's delight he was a natural. School was about to begin again, and the coach had started practicing with the team to get them all back in shape and familiar again with the plays. Linda had smiled, thinking of how proud they were of all their children.

"So, where is he?" Luke asked as he drove up and into the driveway.

"He should be here any minute," she stated very matter-of-factly. The girls had gymnastic lessons that day, so every once in a while Aidan would ride his bike to the field because of the conflict. He had told her many times that there were other boys who also rode their bikes to practice. As usual, he would normally arrive right after practice and just in time for dinner. Why would that night be any different? But it was.

For hours after his expected arrival came and went, they had frantically called their neighbors and then finally police. They had called the coach and parents of the boys he usually rode his bike with. No one had seen anything. It was as if Aidan had simply disappeared into the night. Linda was so distraught that Luke chose to watch Riley and Raney as the officers collected what information they needed to begin the search.

"What do you mean you don't consider him a missing person for twenty-four hours!" Linda retorted incredulously.

"Normally, kids his age usually wind up being found at a friend's house or trying to run away or something. We wouldn't want to have a lot of paperwork and manpower out on a search that might be pointless."

"I know my son, officer, and this isn't like him."

"Yes, ma'am, I understand what you're saying, but kids are kids. Chances are he was just playing video games a little too long with one of his buddies and lost track of time."

Linda knew better. Something inside of her knew instinctively that Aidan was in danger. Even if the officers did not believe her. "Like I told you before, officer, I know something's wrong, and all I'm asking you to do is help us find our boy. He's a good kid and should've been home hours ago. I've called his friends and their parents and no one has seen him. I'm telling you somebody has our boy. I can't explain it but I know in my heart that if he is not here it is not by his choice." Linda wiped the tears away from her face as she spoke.

Luke had overheard her comments and was trying very hard not to allow his own emotions to show in front of the girls. They were already afraid and asking questions that he did not know the answers to.

"We will do the best we can and assure you that everything will be okay."

Linda blinked back more tears as she nodded to the officers and handed them the most recent photo of Aidan. "Please," she whispered, "please find my boy." After answering a few more questions, she closed the door and walked into the living room.

Luke had put on a movie for the girls to watch and walked into the living room to be with Linda. Both instinctively ran into each other's arms feeling hopeless, helpless, and overwhelmed.

"Honey, we need to pray," Luke said, and they bowed their heads. Both had been up most of the evening, hoping that a phone call would end the nightmare, but it never came. Eventually, sunlight streamed through the blinds and forced them to acknowledge that a new day had come. He had called his work and she the church and family members. Thankfully, everyone was agreeable to looking for Aidan, and the Sunday school class had even offered to make flyers.

Both knew that time was of the essence. Linda and Luke continued to call their friends and family for support. The story had now reached the local media station, and the police department was about to start their search through the parks in the city and go door to door to the residences where Aidan might have ridden his bike that day had he been on his way home.

It was the beginning of another day with no new information, and Luke and Linda were still beside themselves with anxiousness and grief, yet both determined to continue the search. Each had stood in front of the cameras pleading for their son and even shown up along with their daughters as the officers and volunteers helped search the parks and other outdoor recreational areas in Taylor, but again with empty hands and heavy hearts. Not even a stitch of clothing had been found.

"Where are you, Aidan?" Linda called out toward the sky as she sat on the front porch.

"What are you doing?" Luke asked, still feeling exhausted from the stress of recent events.

"I'm just calling out his name. I keep thinking he is gonna come riding up the driveway on his bike and tell us that this was all some big joke, you know. And I would get angry for a minute and then hug and kiss him 'cause I knew everything was all right." Linda angrily brushed back her hair away from her face, the lack of sleep beginning to show.

"Linda, I know. Everybody is doing everything they can. I want him home too, but I don't know what else to do."

"I know, I just want him here now. Like a normal day with the kids going up and down the stairs and playing together while I wash the dishes after dinner. I can't stand not knowing if he's okay or not. This is killing me," Linda said sadly as she leaned into Luke and buried her face deep into his chest, sobbing without abandon. Luke held her tightly trying so hard to be her strong, unwavering husband. But truth be known, he was just as ready to burst into his tears as she. This was his son too, and he wanted him back as well as answers to why someone would do such a thing. But for now he needed to let her grieve and be there for her despite his own feelings.

A few minutes passed and then they both looked up to see Raney and Riley staring in the doorway. Raney was the first to speak. "We were just worried where you were." Both were in their pajamas and holding on to their favorite stuffed animals. *It must be hard on them too*, Linda thought, and she stretched out her arm to beckon them to come and join them.

The girls instantly ran at the sight of an open invitation toward Luke and Linda. Each one hugging one another, closing their eyes with hopes that all of this would soon end and life would feel, once again, as if it were moving forward. The wind blew against them as they held each other fiercely. Linda was the first to look up and bring her arms down.

"We need to pray harder, Luke. Something tells me we need to pray right now." Luke looked at Linda. Her eyes were swollen from the tears and the mascara had smeared across her face, but something inside of him could feel the desperate plea resonating.

"All right, honey. We'll pray. Do you wanna go inside?" Luke glanced at the door.

"No, I want to pray right here. Right in our front yard, right where I am, please Luke." He turned back toward her and the girls.

"Okay," he said, looking around to see if any of the neighbors were watching. *They probably think we're nuts*, Luke thought. He grabbed the girls' hands, bowed his head, and each took a turn praying aloud.

One of the lights came on across the street, then another. Luke tried not to be distracted, but soon more lights had turned on.

"Hey, Mr. Williams, is everything all right over there?"

"Yes, we're fine," Luke said, looking up after they had finished. He and Linda watched as their neighbors turned off their lights and stepped back into their houses, some of them shaking their heads in confusion, others opening their blinds, still curious at the strange behavior.

Linda brushed off her clothes seemingly unperturbed and ushered the girls back inside. Luke followed, still glancing back to see if their neighbors had finally realized they were inside for the night. *No need to peer out of their windows now*, he surmised as he sat down on the sofa. Linda had already gone upstairs to comfort the girls and put them to bed. The television had remained on since the night of Aidan's disappearance and Luke sat glued to the news with anticipation of any new developments. Only a repeat of an earlier segment played, with a follow up from the broadcaster that no new evidence had been presented about the matter but that anyone with information was to call.

Luke looked at the screen in disgust. He knew that the officers were investigating, but it felt like they were dragging their feet. "No new leads," he said aloud sarcastically. He knew he had no right to be angry, but ever since Aidan's disappearance every different type of emotion had coursed through his mind making his body feel drained. Taylor was a nice, quiet town without too vast a population. How could no one have seen anything? How could this happen in such a pleasant community? It wasn't like this was New York or anything. Luke continued to shake his head feeling as if he wasn't doing enough either.

Linda walked down the stairs to see him sitting there on the couch, his head between his hands as if thinking. She knew he was just as frustrated and worn as she was. The detective and other officers had simply told them to stay put. But they both knew that the department did not understand the gravity of the situation. Linda could see in their eyes that they had figured he simply ran away or was being belligerent. But she could sense Aidan's danger. She herself had led a few of the searches in the neighborhood, but with no results; everyone just seemed to drift back into their own lives. The calls were still coming to convey sympathy, but the fact was that the whole entire town could not stop their jobs and lives to only focus on their son. The local news station was continuing to run the segments of their son's disappearance, and the officers had continued to assure them that the investigation was still ongoing and that they would be following up on any new leads. Luke had even offered to extend a cash reward, which the detective thought was a good idea. But . . . still nothing and the continued feeling of helplessness felt more and more prevalent as another day was about to come and go without any news of Aidan.

"The girls are asleep . . . finally," Linda said, sitting down beside him on the sofa.

"That's good," he said. "I know they are upset and confused too. Sleep is something I'm really beginning to miss." He rubbed his eyes tiredly.

"I know, me too," she said, "but I wanna be ready the second that phone rings and they tell me that he is fine."

Luke paused for a moment letting her words sink in before he spoke. "What if the call doesn't come, Linda?"

She looked at him angrily, the tears starting to form. "What do you mean?"

"You know well what I mean. What if we never know, what if he never comes home?" Luke felt the lump in his throat as he spoke.

"He'll be okay. Don't talk like that. He is GONNA COME HOME," Linda said emphatically, folding her arms together as if this were something she had control over. Even she knew this was a possibility, but she still had hope that he was alive and okay. That thought was crucial at this moment because the other alternative would devastate her very senses.

"Please don't ever say that again to me," her eyes pleading with him.

"Honey, I'm not saying it to upset you and the Lord knows there is nothing I want more than my son home, my wife happy, and our family back together. But these last few days have brought a situation in our lives that we couldn't have even fathomed, and only God knows why. As much as I will never give up hope in finding him, I must still recognize that it may be that we don't and that we may have to pick up the pieces and still exist as a family. I know you don't wanna hear a single word I'm saying and believe me . . . I get it . . . I just want you to be realistic."

"I *am* being realistic, Luke. You sound like you just want to give up trying to find him," she said, her voice faltering.

"Oh really?" he said, her words still stinging. "You know that's not true, Linda. I feel just as helpless as you sitting in this house not knowing when to come and go or even where to. It's my job to protect you and the kids, and I can't even do that." Luke slumped down further into the sofa realizing that perhaps he had spoken too harshly. Linda stared at him and burst into tears. She jumped up and began to pace the floor.

"I just can't quit crying, Luke. I can't sleep, I can't eat, I can't even think straight anymore."

"And you think I can?" Luke asked, staring down at her, his own eyes wet with tears. "He is OUR boy, and I do know how you feel even if I have a different way of expressing it. We will get through this and we will do it together."

Linda smiled back at him and he motioned to her to sit back down.

"Come sit with me," Luke said, "I know you don't plan on just walking back and forth in the living room until daybreak do you?"

"No."

"Well then come sit by me," Luke said, patting the sofa cushion. Linda walked toward him and sat down. Perhaps just a moment or two to get off her feet was a good idea so she slipped off her shoes and let her toes stretch out as she yawned.

"See, doesn't that feel just a little bit better?" Luke said.

"Yes, but I don't wish to sit too long. I need to go get my cell phone and have it handy. I'll just sit a few minutes," she said, tiredly closing her eyes. But the minutes quickly turned to hours and their exhausted bodies demanded what they refused to give it—rest.

"Mom, Dad, wake up it's morning." Linda looked up to see Riley tugging on her hand. She awoke abruptly, inwardly upset at having drifted to sleep for so long. Glancing upward she noticed her husband still sleeping with his head tilted awkwardly against the arm of the sofa.

"Hi, baby," Linda said, smiling at Riley. "Is Raney up?"

"Yep, she's at the table and said she is hungry. So, I told her that I would come wake you up so we could have some breakfast."

"Okay, I can do that, but let's be real quiet so as not to wake Daddy." Linda grabbed Riley's hand and both tiptoed into the kitchen where Raney sat eagerly for them to appear.

"Mom," Raney said loudly. Linda put her finger to her mouth whispering to her to hush.

"Daddy is still sleeping and I know he really needs it, so let's do our best to be quiet for now and I'll start making something for you both to eat." Just as she began to pull the eggs out of the refrigerator the cell phone in her purse began to ring loudly. Linda dropped the eggs on the floor in a panic as she ran toward her purse to answer the phone before it stopped ringing.

4

The Taylor Police Department was unusually busy since the night of Aidan's disappearance. However, most of the calls coming in the last few days had been more of a deterrence than helpful. Not a single real lead had developed, leaving Detective Stearns to shake his head in confusion. It was as if this kid had just vanished into thin air. *Hard for me to believe no one saw a thing,* he thought. He had been a detective for twelve years. Not yet something to brag about, but he'd seen a few things here and there, which made him no longer a rookie. At thirty-nine years of age, his blond hair and light green eyes made him look more like a surfer than someone in law enforcement. But after college, instead of pursuing other ventures like his roommates, he had chosen to move back to Taylor and sign on with the police department. Taylor was as most towns with a decent population and good ole Southern charm— the idyllic town that everyone either wanted to raise kids in or peacefully grow old. Something like this happening just seemed unheard of, like a sick hoax to get everyone up in arms. But after personally interviewing Luke and Linda Williams it was more than apparent this was not the case.

They were a middle-aged couple with three kids. No criminal background, solid citizens, and churchgoers. And from the sound of it, there were no conflicts going on with their son, Aidan. Seemed like a normal kid. No enemies, no bullies at school, no behavioral issues at all. Basically, no motive. As happy as he was that the family environment had been good, it left open the real possibility that someone had taken him, and that meant that not only was this kid in danger but others were as well. The thought caused him to shiver as he propped himself up and leaned all the way back in his chair to allow his mind to delve more into that line of thinking. Officers and quite a few volunteers had searched all of the parks in the area and visited with friends, neighbors, and family of the Williamses in order to question them for new evidence. But nothing other than a few speculations had popped up. Detective Stearns knew he needed something solid and was having difficulty pinning down a reason or an individual. The alerts to most police departments within their vicinity had been utilized and each department had been notified of the dire situation and the ever-growing pressure to find the boy.

For once, Detective Stearns was completely baffled. Patrol cars had continued to monitor anything and anyone who looked suspicious, and the media had also continued to run a segment of his disappearance, but with very little success. The Williamses had even gone as far as to make flyers and had others post them in various locations as well as offer a cash reward for his safe return, which the detective had thought a good idea. He had indicated to Mr. Williams that in the past, money had usually persuaded people to call the police department. Mr. Williams had inquired as to why that was and why didn't someone just call because it's the right thing to do. Detective Stearns smiled at Mr. Williams' lack of understanding but was saddened as he explained that in his experience, there had been instances where additional information had been needed and it was only received after the reward had been announced.

What a shame, he had thought to himself, knowing that a man's son had just been kidnapped should require no more incentive than that to see that justice was served. He tried to adjust his chair as he maneuvered his feet, but the chair kept rolling and he put his feet back down on the floor. He pulled out a map of Taylor and, beginning at city hall, he suggested that search teams split up in order to cover more ground and report to the department any new discoveries. Mrs. Williams had also provided a pair of clothes that had been recently worn by her son so that the canines could be used in the search and rescue operations. There had been no sexual offenders within a ten-mile radius and those who were listed on the register had been compliant in allowing the detective and his fellow law enforcement officers to search their homes. Everyone seemed to be cooperative.

Still, there was obviously something missing. Detective Maris Stearns believed there was no such thing as a "perfect crime." Sooner or later, a fingerprint, a piece of clothing, or a misguided step would lead them further in their investigation. "My job is never easy," he grimaced, looking at the database for the town and surrounding areas. Perhaps he wasn't searching the way he should, and he closed his eyes remembering the words of his college professor when a question had stumped him in his last semester. "It's not about the problem, but your approach." That comment had prompted him to study differently and "approach" each problem in various ways or methods. Maybe this was one of those times. This case was different and a new strategy needed to be formed, as every minute was crucial.

"Detective," a voice called out, and Stearns looked up.

"You got a phone call from Chief Roberts. Says he needs to speak with you about the missing kid."

Detective Stearns quickly grabbed the phone and his pen. Pushing a few items off his desk, he located a legal pad and pressed the button to be connected. "Chief Roberts, Stearns speaking."

"Stearns, first let me congratulate you on your twelve years at Taylor. Most fellows would have died by now."

"Come again, sir? I don't understand. Died?"

"Yes, of boredom," he said, laughing as if his sense of sarcasm had been funny.

"Ha ha," Stearns said forcefully, clearly not amused.

Chief Vince "Bear Paw" Roberts as everyone called him was nothing short of an egotistical bully, who no doubt had never been confronted by someone who wasn't easily intimidated. Stearns had surmised that most people either let it go or thought it better to just let him ramble. As a kid, he had always heard that Chief Roberts had gotten his nickname from coming into contact with a bear while on a hunting expedition up north with some of his cohorts, but the real truth was probably that he had gotten into some sort of fight and felt embarrassed having been cut across the face. Stearns wanted to comment but thought it better to maintain civility.

"Thought you called to talk about the missing boy, Chief."

"I did," Chief Roberts said, drawing in a deep breath as he spoke.

"Yeah, well I'm listening," Detective Stearns said as he closed his door and put the speakerphone on.

"Good, I've been keeping a lookout for you ever since we got word about the situation, and I take it that you have no leads so far, right?"

"Right," Stearns said with disappointment.

"Tell me what you have done so far," Chief Roberts said and waited for Detective Stearns to speak.

Stearns began with his visit with Mr. & Mrs. Williams, the research, searched areas, etc.

"Any persons of interest?" Chief Roberts asked after a moment of silence.

"No, Chief, we ruled out the parents, other family members, and the kid had no enemies or anyone that would wanna cause harm. We even spoke with the sex offenders registered in Taylor, and all of them were reasonably cooperative and had alibis for the night of the boy's disappearance. I mean, I just don't get it. One minute the kid is coming back from practice and then swoosh, he's gone."

"You say you searched all the parks, but what about other wooded areas?"

"What do you mean, Chief? Like some of those areas that are wooded on the outskirts of Taylor?"

"Yep, did you send your guys out there to make sure you weren't missing anything?"

"No, not really," Detective Stearns said.

"Then, I suggest you look."

"Why is that, Chief? Something you know that you need to let me in on?"

"I'm gonna just let you know that before you moved back to Taylor and with the department we had a situation not unlike what you're dealing with now."

"WHAT! You've gotta be joking, Chief," Stearns said incredulously. "Why didn't you call me before this?"

"Stearns, I wasn't gonna call you about all this in the event a kid was just wanting to be rebellious and not come home for dinner. Once I realized you hadn't found the boy, it made me recall an old case I had worked on when I was younger where a young boy had been kidnapped not far from his house here in Green Valley. Nobody had seemed to know anything, and we didn't have the manpower then like we do now."

"So, what happened?"

"Sad turn of events, I'm afraid," Chief Roberts said, pausing for a moment.

"Well, I'm listening. Explain." Detective Stearns was not one to be toyed with simply for theatrical effect. He liked answers and quickly.

"We finally found the body of the ten-year-old boy in a wooded area about a week after we were notified of his disappearance. It appeared he had been stabbed multiple times, and his feet and hands had been bound. What's worse is that when we notified the mother, we also had to tell her that he had been sexually abused."

Detective Stearns winced and shook his head in obvious disgust. "Tell me you caught the creep that did that."

Chief Roberts cleared his throat. "No, that's the thing, we never did. The ropes were analyzed, but they were so common anyone could have used them, and back then we weren't able to analyze DNA like now. Oddly enough, the most we could identify was that it was a male, probably late teens, early twenties, and that he probably had a criminal past due to his meticulous moves to avoid detection and identification. We interviewed a few locals and a couple of outsiders who were new to town, but everyone checked out. After a while the case just turned cold, and we filed it away. That case haunted me for years 'cause nothing like that had ever happened, and since then nothing like it has. Pretty sure the boy's mother is still upset about it also, but we never did catch the person responsible for such a heinous crime. But this particular missing person you got now seems to be eerily similar to that old murder, and I'd like to see you catch whoever it is and bring 'em to justice."

"I'm trying, Chief. Sounds like I'm running into the same problem as you did, and with nothing new, I've exhausted my options. Although, you did say to extend the search, which I will do as quickly as possible. But it sounds like it may be too late. Think I should make a phone call to the Williamses and at the very least let them know about this."

"You got kids, Detective?"

"No, why?"

"'Cause you need to put yourself in a parents' shoes when you tell them things like this or worse. You have to tell them that their kid is not coming back."

"I don't want to have to tell them that. I want to catch this guy and bring this kid safely back to his family. I would appreciate any insight you can give me from now on as well as letting me get a look at that old file."

"I can do that," Chief Roberts said, his voice getting thick. "But I want something in return."

Detective Stearns grimaced trying to figure out what Chief Roberts might possibly want from him. "Whatcha want, Chief? Although, seems like you would want to be helpful no matter what . . . right?"

"Oh, sure," he said, sounding disingenuous. "I just wanna little of the praise if you do catch this guy. You know a little bit of glory for ole' Bear Paw. I've been thinking of running for political office here in Green Valley and something like that would help out my campaign."

Stearns wasn't sure if he wanted to burst out laughing at such a blatant request or just hang up on such a pathetic glory hound. Pausing for a moment, he realized that despite his distaste for Chief Roberts' antics, his expertise and knowledge would prove helpful.

44

"Sure thing, Chief," he said, trying not to sound too sarcastic. "Just don't forget to send me what you've got on that cold case. There might be something in there that could help me out, so the sooner the better."

"Understood," Chief Roberts said, calling out to one of his deputies.

Detective Stearns could hear the chief barking his orders before he hung up the phone and smiled. Even if the chief's name would be all over the headlines, it ultimately didn't matter. His focus was on the missing boy, and it was going to stay there. He grabbed the phone again and quickly dialed the number in his pocket.

"Hello?"

"Hi, Mrs. Williams, this is Detective Stearns." The phone got quiet. "Mrs. Williams?"

"Yes, yes I'm here," she said, sounding tired.

"Would you and Mr. Williams be able to meet me at the police department tomorrow? Say 10:00 a.m.?"

"Is something wrong, Detective?"

"Just got some information from the chief of police in Green Valley, though I don't have any new information about your son, Aidan. What I can tell you is that the recent conversation with the chief may shed some light on this case and may provide us with more info while we continue our efforts to find your boy. So, can you and your husband come by?"

"Of course, we have our two daughters, but if it is at 10:00 a.m., they should be visiting with some friends of ours from church. They offered to help watch them in the event we needed them to. So, yes, we will most definitely be there."

After everyone had ended the call, Detective Stearns paced for a half hour in his office debating on how to proceed with the recent news from Chief Roberts. A knock on the door jolted his thoughts, and he motioned for the deputy from Green Valley to come in.

"Man, that was fast. What did ya do, fly over here?"

"No," the deputy replied laughing. "When the chief gives an order we'd best do what he says. He told me that you had to have it today and that I'd best get moving. So, I did."

Detective Stearns managed a smile as he took the file from the deputy's hands. It looked large and disorganized, so he laid it down on his desk, still closed.

"Guess you'd best be headed back, but tell Chief Roberts thanks."

"Will do, Detective. Me and the boys are gonna be on the lookout for anything suspicious. So, no worries. If I see something I'll tell the chief to call you."

Detective Stearns nodded his appreciation as the deputy left his office. Sitting down at his desk, he opened up the large file and began perusing through the documents. The file was very much in disarray and nothing was really placed in an orderly fashion. Photos were scattered haphazardly throughout the file, and he decided after a few moments that the first thing he needed to do was lay everything out in stacks on his desk and then review them all. First, he stacked the correspondence in one pile. Second, he stacked the medical reports including the coroner's report. The third consisted of statements and investigative research. The fourth stack was of photos, and the last pile was for miscellaneous items that might have not fit nicely in one of the other stacks. This process took over an hour as he quickly glanced over each document and set it in the appropriate pile. After he was finished sorting the entire file material, he stood up to stretch his legs for a moment and requested that he not be disturbed unless it involved the disappearance or was an emergency. He then went and locked his door, turning back to the file material in front of him. Even various newspaper clippings were scattered about and had made their way to the detective's miscellaneous stack.

Detective Stearns began reading each and every document, making notes as he reviewed everything on his desk. When he finally got to the stack of photos, it was painful to go through. A couple were of the little boy smiling—probably provided by the mother from the looks of it—and then there were others obviously showing the lifeless body before it had been moved in order to preserve any evidence. Stearns was not squeamish when it came to blood or dead bodies, but the decaying corpse of a young boy stabbed, bound, and gagged was almost too much. *Hopefully, the child's mother did not see these photographs*, he thought as he closed his eyes, knowing full well that this image was now seared in his mind whether he wanted it to be or not. Detective Stearns put down the photos and searched the documents for the coroner's report. The report had given the time of death in the a.m. Early a.m. *Interesting*, he thought as he wrote that down with a few comments. Death due to blood loss it further noted but implied that there were other traces of assault on the body, specifically on the face. Again, Detective Stearns continued to make notes and comments. The report itself was long and thorough, showing the body outline with marks or notations for every place that there had been some type of assault or questionable marking that did not appear to be self-inflicted.

Detective Stearns tried to imagine what it must have been like for that small boy, but he could not. The fear that must have gripped him and the pain that he probably endured up to his death was too sad to think about. Chief Roberts had even mentioned that he had been sexually abused, a thought that simply revolted him to the point of anger. If this murderer was still on the loose and somehow had something to do with his case, he was determined to expose this individual for who and what he was—a monster. After another hour of reviewing and making notes, he sipped on his coffee and let out a yawn. He needed to begin organizing another group of volunteers and a couple of deputies to go search the wooded areas that separated Taylor from the town of Green Valley. He knew that many would help; he just needed to get on the phone and start coordinating who and when.

Picking up the phone, he dialed the local newspaper.

"Hello, Taylor Tribune," a woman's pleasant voice said.

"Hello . . . this is Detective Stearns. I have a question or two to ask you. Not sure if you would have anything archived regarding the death of a boy named Tanner McKenzie some time back?"

"Oh goodness," the lady answered back politely. "It may take me a while, but I'm pretty sure that I saved a few articles. I was working here when that happened, so I'm fairly certain that the newspaper articles were kept, considering the disappearance and all . . ." her voice trailing off slightly.

"I would appreciate anything you can provide me," Detective Stearns replied as he explained who he was.

"I'm sure we can accommodate you, Detective. Just ask for me, Ethel, if you don't get what you need in a couple of days. I'll start working on it right now."

Detective Stearns hung up the phone feeling slightly queasy as he thought of the meeting with the Williamses. Although he had initially welcomed the thought of letting them know where things were in the investigation, he was not too keen on trying to answer the more serious questions that they may pose to him, such as their son's welfare and the probability of his safe return. Unfortunately, this was an area he was not well equipped to handle. So far, he had managed to get by, but now he wasn't so sure. They were going to ask tough questions and who could blame them? The longer it took to catch this individual the less likely their son was alive and that would have to be addressed, no matter how painful. Although there was no concrete evidence that this disappearance and the murder from long ago were orchestrated by the same individual, the similarities were strikingly familiar. But if it was the same individual, then Aidan Williams was probably lying in some ditch just waiting for someone to find his lifeless body.

He stared again at the photos and kept feeling like there were clues in them, but his mind kept drawing a blank. "Maybe I just need to get some sleep," he said to himself. Closing the files on his desk, he tidied up his office and grabbed his car keys. Once out of the office, he figured he'd ride down toward the wooded area that spanned about a hundred acres separating a portion of the towns of Taylor and Green Valley. Some of the area had been purchased and a park built a couple of years ago. Initially, they had searched the park itself and hadn't found even a trace of the bicycle that the Williamses claimed their son was riding at the time of his abduction. It wasn't yet dark, so even though police officers had patrolled most of these areas nonstop, it wouldn't hurt to just go check it out for himself. Maybe sit for a moment and clear his head.

The idea sounded like a good one. He quickly made a left after exiting onto Main Street with his window down and his radio blaring. Maris Stearns was trying hard not to let the pressure of solving this case overwhelm him. But even with the wind in his face and beautiful scenery, not much in his mind had changed. The fact that he wasn't cramped up in that little office behind his desk was a good thing, but it wasn't much of a difference when it came to his thoughts. His mind and heart were racing and until he had more answers, neither one was about to let up and give him any peace. He figured after he talked to the Williamses, he would go and meet with the lady who had lost her son in the Green Valley case and arrange for a team of officers and volunteers to search the wooded area as Chief Roberts had suggested. The traffic wasn't too bad and before long Stearns was on the outskirts of town and plodding toward his destination. As he suspected, the ride had been a good choice. He was able to collect his thoughts, and with the next day no doubt being an emotional one, now was the time to have solitude and quiet reflection.

Although Aidan Williams was a bit older, both abducted children, Stearns had read, were good kids. No behavioral problems and no real reason that they had been singled out except to say they had ventured away from their friends and parents just long enough to be vulnerable. "What a shame," he said, recalling his own childhood and how much he had enjoyed riding his bike around his old neighborhood. His mother hadn't given him too much grief about riding around for hours because every kid knew each other and would go up and down the road until it got dark or until somebody's mother called out that it was dinnertime.

"Can't do that these days," he said to himself sadly. Despite the tranquility of a town like Taylor, this was proof that even it was not impervious to the crimes of larger cities or strangers that seemed to be popping up left and right. He parked his truck and stepped out, looking around. The area was unusually quiet, but he wasn't surprised. Although the town had resumed the normal hustle and bustle, many of the familiar spots for children had been abandoned until there were more answers to the recent kidnapping. The swing sets were empty and the picnic tables stood abandoned. Detective Stearns sat down at one not far from his vehicle. The view was perfect as he scanned the area. The woods were approximately a hundred yards away and within a short walk. He debated walking through them but thought better of it. *If Chief Roberts is right, someone very dangerous could be lurking in there and it might not be safe to just walk around haphazardly. Best to simply wait until I have the resources to search the area thoroughly.* Looking once more into the trees he got into his vehicle and drove off. He couldn't shake the feeling like he was leaving something behind, or perhaps someone. He stared in the rearview mirror until he could no longer see the trees fading away in the distance, determined to find Aidan Williams one way or another.

5

Anna McKenzie sat in her chair staring sadly at her television. She knew it was simply a matter of time before they would be calling her about her boy, Tanner. *Oh, Tanner,* she thought, pulling the blanket up and around her frail shoulders. *My beautiful, beautiful boy, why did you have to be taken from me?* It was almost unbearable, but as time passed, things had gotten a little easier. However, with the recent child abduction, it was like it was happening all over again and everything felt as fresh and as raw as the day it had happened to her and her life was suddenly changed forever. Sure, she had tried to seek counseling but ended up trying to cope on her own, preferring to be left alone than to drain her wallet and sit on some stranger's chair. Back then she had been a single mom and though things were tight back then, she and Tanner had always managed to make do and be happy for what they had. His infectious laugh always caused her to smile and be encouraged, even when she would sometimes think about his father and how, in a drunken rage, he had left them penniless, never returning. She recalled when he would ask her about him she would simply reply that "Daddy has lost his way and perhaps one day he would find it." She meant it metaphorically of course—to represent his spirituality with God—but little Tanner had taken it seriously. Sometimes he even left the flashlight on long after he had fallen asleep in the unlikely event that Daddy might need a light so he could see his way home. Anna had chosen to not fuss at him about it, and for a while it had become the norm, that is until he had gotten older and more aware of things.

"Dad's not ever coming back, is he?" he had said, coming inside the house after school one afternoon.

"What makes you say such a thing?" she had asked, looking into his sad eyes.

"Mom, for years when I was little with my flashlight, you never once told me that he wasn't coming back and probably never wanted to."

"Well, that's not entirely true. I might have doubted your father's return; however, anything is possible with God. I admired your tenacity to never give up on your father. God doesn't work on the same time frame as we do. Just because we want things and want them right now, it doesn't mean that we are just going to instantly get what we desire."

Tanner had nodded his agreement, but it was still evident that he had been too young to understand such a complex thought, and his heart was still left feeling crushed with no father figure to look up to and ask questions that only "guys" could answer.

Anna had kept quiet trying to do her best to play both roles in the house, but it was not easy and definitely no substitute. As Tanner got older, he stopped asking altogether about his father and she didn't bring it up. He was a beautiful child and very well behaved. It didn't take much effort to instantly fall in love with him. At ten, he had been so eager to make new friends in the neighborhood and join some of the sporting events that when he had asked her, she had immediately caved.

Green Valley was a close-knit community, and she didn't really see the harm in him getting out of the house for a few hours during the day and enjoying himself. At the time she thought that was exactly what he needed, and she was hard pressed to tell him no. Regrettably, it had only been a few months after that in which he had been taken from her, and his budding life was suddenly and tragically cut short. A wave of nausea caught her abruptly as she was thinking. She tried to lean her head back until it passed. Unfortunately, this was a common occurrence whenever she let her mind travel to that time and those feelings. As long as she thought of him before then, she was okay, but if she let her mind wander to that day and the ones immediately following after, she would feel listless all over again and get sick.

Feelings of regret, sadness, and anger would course through her without control. It was a pain indescribable—the emptiness, the ache, the unanswered questions forever looming. For weeks she had struggled to get out of bed, the house in disarray, his worn shoes still scattered near the front door where he would take them off from playing outside. Nothing had seemed worth getting out of the house for. People had stopped by to give their condolences, but she had still felt like a ghost wandering through the flurry of people. After the media had left town and everyone finally had resumed their own lives, she was able to grieve quietly, personally. His room remained the same, but it had been a while since she had walked in there, a sure sign that she was trying to let him go and move on with her life. But staring at the news, the fragile existence she was in was one step away from crumbling.

Something inside her gave her the chills. She could not explain it but somehow she knew that every second was crucial in finding this boy, that is, if his family did not want him to end up like hers. She wondered if Chief "Bear Paw" remembered her boy. He had been the one who had driven up in his patrol car to tell her that Tanner was found. At first, she had been elated until she saw the look in his tired eyes, realizing it wasn't anything to be happy about. She recalled his arms catching her as she collapsed, the magnitude of his words causing her to feel numb and lifeless.

He had stayed with her until her neighbor had gotten home and offered to help. Though usually, he had a way of coming across as pompous, she knew there was more to him than that. She'd seen it, felt his sympathy when her whole world had collapsed. *This poor boy's mother*, she thought, looking again at the television as a picture of Aidan Williams stared back at her. He looked like a nice kid, like her Tanner. Happy, eager, athletic, and full of potential. The tears slowly fell and she held the blanket tightly as they dropped. She was so used to them that it seemed so pointless to even brush them away, knowing full well that she would wind up brushing more away. She knew they had not found this little boy yet and that the search was still ongoing.

Perhaps they were missing something. The Green Valley Police Department had done the same things but finally they ended up with nothing and her with a dead son. Though she knew now that they had done everything they could, initially there was blame in her mind to go around, perhaps because she needed something or someone to focus her feelings of anger on. She did not have the satisfaction of looking at her son's murderer in his face behind bars. She had blamed herself for letting him go and blamed the cops for not finding him in town, but all of that was the wrong way to think and she knew that now.

She knew that only he was to blame. This sadistic, evil individual with no face and no name. Was he back? Was he the one who had taken another little boy away from his mother? The circumstances were too similar. When nothing had happened after Tanner had been murdered in Green Valley, people had just figured the guy had split and probably crossed the border to avoid prosecution. The years of peacefulness in the community afterward had supported that idea until now. Taylor was a different town, of course, but still close. Her stomach began to feel queasy as a thought crept into her head. *Maybe he had never left. Maybe he's been here all this time, just waiting for someone else to take.*

Anna jumped out of her seat, tossing the blanket to the side as she ran to the bathroom. She felt better once she had emptied her stomach. Sitting back down in her chair tiredly, she pulled the blanket back up and covered herself as she felt chills and jumped slightly when she heard the phone ring.

"Yes?"

"Is this Ms. Anna . . . Anna McKenzie?"

"Who is this? What do you want?" Anna asked, not recognizing the man's voice.

"Ms. McKenzie, this is Detective Maris Stearns from the Taylor Police Department. Would it be okay to speak with you and ask you a few questions regarding your late son Tanner?"

"Late son, huh? Just son will do," she snapped back.

"Ma'am I didn't mean to offend you," Detective Stearns said quickly.

"I know you didn't. I would just prefer that you not say that to me. Just address him as Tanner."

"Yes ma'am," Stearns said apologetically. "May I speak to you about Tanner?"

"I figured y'all would be calling me sooner or later now that this other kid got taken like my boy."

"So you think there are some similarities, ma'am?" Stearns asked rather abruptly.

"And you don't?" she replied sarcastically. "Seein' as how you are calling me, you *must* be thinking that also. In fact, I was just sittin' here watching the news and wondering when you boys were gonna come out and talk to me, not where, not why, but when. Does that answer your question?"

Detective Stearns was a bit surprised by her hostility, but he knew by her comments that she was still mourning her son and possibly holding on to some deep-seated resentment. He had to be patient and hopefully she would understand that he was not trying to rudely invade her life or bring up such a painful event for no reason. Although her son was dead, perhaps she could shed some light on the investigation now and save another child from the same fate as her son's. He chose his words carefully, taking a long pause before speaking.

"Ms. McKenzie, I am very sorry for your loss. I know that seeing all of this now has probably brought up some painful memories, and I assure you I do not, and did not, mean to upset you or offend you in *any* way. As you no doubt are aware, I have been placed in charge of this investigation. We spoke to the parents of the missing boy and have conducted searches in and around Taylor . . . but with no real leads our window of opportunity to save this child from his captor is quickly closing. I was at my wits end until I got a phone call from Chief Roberts telling me about a case a long time ago involving your son. Both he and I have reason to believe that the abduction of Aidan Williams and Tanner were very similar and may, in fact, be carried out by the same individual. There is no proof of this theory yet, but if we are correct, then this man is armed and dangerous, and the likelihood of that young boy being alive is less than 50 percent. I am hoping there is something that you might know that could help. Perhaps a recollection of the events leading up to your son's disappearance might have some bearing as to the m.o. of this individual. For one, I will say that he does not pick them solely on their looks because your boy and the recent one look nothing alike. However, they were both about the same age and same build. The boy in Taylor was riding his bike, which we still have not recovered. Was your son walking or riding his bike?"

"He was walking."

"Where was he walking to?"

"He was walking home." Anna started to sob softly.

"Ma'am, I did not mean to make you cry. Would you prefer I talk to you some other time?"

"Yes, maybe tomorrow morning," Anna said, feeling grateful that she could be left alone for the moment.

"Okay, Ms. McKenzie, I'll call you tomorrow morning. Good-bye and thank you for your time."

Detective Stearns hung up the phone not knowing if this line of questioning would actually lead to anything, but he knew he needed to try, that is, if Ms. McKenzie was willing. Clearly, she was not in an emotional state to discuss it. *Man*, he thought, *even after all these years, she is still in mourning. How sad.*

The Williamses would be coming to the office soon, and he wanted to provide them with some hope. The file on the deceased boy, Tanner, was still in his office, so he decided while he was waiting for them he would open it back up and try to analyze everything again now that he had slept well the night before. Reading over the autopsy report again, he almost didn't hear the door open and Mr. and Mrs. Williams step inside.

He quickly grabbed the photos that were strewn about, shoving them hurriedly into the file. That was the last thing he wanted them to see.

"I apologize, I was just going over some evidence on another case," he said, combing his hair back with his hand and motioning for them to have a seat.

Normally, his office was neat and well organized, but as of late his paperwork was piling up and empty coffee cups littered his desk and credenza. A few maps of the town were hung up on a large easel with red dots for all the places that had been searched. He noticed the Williamses staring at it and then looking away. He knew they were becoming worn with no new information. Neither looked like they had slept, and Mrs. Williams' eyes were swollen and dark.

"Mr. and Mrs. Williams, I called you down here to go over what we know and to—"

Luke cut him off. "Just what is that exactly?" the comment somewhat sarcastic.

Detective Stearns bit his lip, realizing the Williams' emotional fragility, and went right back to where he had been interrupted.

"—to tell you that we have marked each and every single place that we have searched and spoken to the owner, resident, or occupant." He pointed to the map that Luke and Linda had stared at earlier. The town of Taylor looked as if it had the chicken pox, with all the red thumb tacks that had been placed in the various locations.

"Do you have any suspects, any ransom notes?" Linda asked, hoping that Detective Stearns had more as to the whereabouts of Aidan.

"No, unfortunately, Mrs. Williams, we have been unable to identify any suspects. Normally we rule out family first, then anyone who could be a potential enemy of the child, like a class bully or anyone who might not have liked him. However, in our investigation, we concurred that there were no domestic or vengeful issues at play. And after speaking with you both at the onset, we also concluded that Aidan was not . . . is not the kinda kid who wants to leave home. So it is with a heavy heart that we must inform you that we believe he was abducted against his will and that he is being held by someone extremely dangerous and probably armed."

"What makes you say that?" Luke Williams asked, feeling like Detective Stearns was holding something back.

"Well, I can't say with certainty, but we have information that makes us believe that that is the case."

"But I thought you said you were unable to identify any suspects? How do you know that whoever took our boy is armed and dangerous?" Linda chimed in, also feeling like there was more.

"Detective Stearns, we have had our only son taken from us. Please, if you know something that you are not telling us, we feel we have a right to know."

Detective Stearns shifted himself in his seat unsure how much he really wanted to say. While he knew and sympathized with them, he didn't want to start discussing another case that he didn't know for sure had any bearing on their situation. "Mrs. Williams," he said, choosing his words carefully, "we simply feel that whoever took your son should be taken seriously and that he is most likely armed. We intend to inform you that we will be searching the woods between Taylor and Green Valley next as we continue to rule out the whereabouts of your son, Aidan."

"Oh, my goodness!" Linda said, putting her hand to her mouth. "Did you say the woods? Does this mean you think he's . . ." Her hands began shaking as Luke put his arms around her.

"No, of course not, but," Detective Stearns said, knowing this was not exactly true, "as you can see by the map just directly behind you, the red pushpins represent the areas where we have been. Those areas did not reveal anything, but our officers continue to patrol those areas. We have decided to expand our search to this area because we received a phone call from the Green Valley Police Department that indicated to me that, quite a few years back, another boy had been abducted and the kidnapper was never found."

"Well, didn't the boy identify him?"

"No, ma'am, the young boy was murdered," Stearns said, swallowing hard as he anticipated a backlash of probing questions.

Luke could see Linda's face turning a lighter shade, and he squeezed her hand. He knew that his wife had left the house with the thought that perhaps they would receive some good news regarding their son, not this. Although he knew that this might be a possibility, he knew that his wife was unwilling to face such a prospect. She was determined to find Aidan and refused to face the reality that the longer the investigation took, the less likely that Aidan would be found alive. They had prayed, of course, for his protection and safe return, but he couldn't help but think about all the stories in far-off cities where the unthinkable happened and left many a family to pick up the pieces of a shattered life.

Linda tried to regain her composure, but it was difficult. The idea of Aidan not riding his bike toward her in their driveway, smiling at her when she helped him with his homework, or holding her hand as they walked into church just seemed so foreign.

"Murdered?" she said, almost whispering.

"Yes, Mrs. Williams. I'm not sure if you recall this particular case or even if you and Mr. Williams were living here in Taylor. A ten-year-old boy was murdered—and I'll be the first to tell you that I don't know all the particulars—but his murder remains unsolved. Because some of the circumstances are alike, we are teaming up with the Green Valley Police Department and heading up a search in that area. It happens to be one of the largest wooded areas in the state, and we are going to need some serious manpower if we are going to search it in its entirety and search it thoroughly. I apologize about my bluntness, but I believe you need to understand that we need to move quickly."

"Have you found any trace of our son thus far? The news keeps saying that there is nothing, and I can't understand how someone could just snatch our boy up like that and not leave a trace. Is something like that even possible?" Luke managed to cough before resuming. "I'm gonna be honest with you when I tell you that we feel like more could be done. Rest assured, I'm not claiming that your department is not doing the best that they can. However, maybe it's not enough, you know. Like maybe we need to call the FBI in and have them use their exhaustive resources to look where we can't. I dunno. We are staying at the house like you told us to do, but we are starting to feel like caged animals." Luke rubbed his bloodshot eyes and put his hands back down in his lap as he waited for Detective Stearns' response. Linda nodded her head as if in agreement with Luke's comments.

Stearns looked at them sadly, not feeling the slightest bit upset at their words. In fact, this was what he had anticipated and prepared himself for. He knew this must be the most trying time of their lives, but he really believed that he and his colleagues were very close to breaking this case wide open. Something inside him indicated that he was on the right path. The problem was he needed to assure them . . . convince them that he would do everything in his power to find their son.

"Mrs. Williams, Mr. Williams, I will do everything I can to find Aidan. If the FBI comes in now, they are simply gonna push us 'underlings' outta the way and then communicate with no one. If you think your lives have been invaded now, just wait. I'm trying to assure you that every single police officer here is doing their level best to find your son as well, and all I'm asking is that you give me a couple more days to follow up with my research on that old case and search those woods. I know that feels like an eternity, but if we still have no leads, then I will relinquish my investigation and call the FBI myself."

Linda looked at Luke as he turned to her, not really sure what to say. Neither one wanted to wait another day without Aidan's safe return, but Detective Stearns made sense, and he had been forthright the entire time. Linda put her hand into Luke's.

"Well, Detective, we appreciate your candor with us and though every day is excruciating to us emotionally, we will wait as you have proposed, but I think I speak for both of us when I tell you that we would also like to help with the search."

Detective Stearns bit his lip, trying to think of the kindest way to tell them that the best thing they could do is wait at home in case he returned and so they would not be . . . in the way. The last thing he wanted was for one of them stumbling on the body of their dead child.

"No, afraid not, it's too risky," he said quickly. "If the kidnapper calls or makes a ransom, I would prefer you both to be at your home."

Linda frowned but she knew she needed to heed the detective's advice. As she and Luke stood up to walk out, the phone rang and they froze. Detective Stearns looked at his phone. The number looked familiar, but he couldn't recall so he picked it up and said hello.

"Detective Stearns? Maris Stearns?" The voice was female, older, and raspy. He instantly recognized it and put his hand up for the Williamses to sit back down.

"Ms. McKenzie, this is Detective Stearns. What can I do for you?"

"Detective, I'm ready to talk to you, and I'd like to help if I can."

6

Maris sat back down in his seat much to the confusion of the Williamses.

"Yes, of course," he said, holding the phone close to his mouth. "I will be there shortly. Yes, yes. I know where Laurel Cove is, yes ma'am of course I will be there. Okay, okay. Bye-bye."

Luke and Linda stared at Detective Stearns, not really sure why he had beckoned them back in but figured it might have something to do with their case and were eager for him to hang up the phone and explain.

Detective Stearns looked up at them. "That was Anna McKenzie, the mother of the slain boy that I was telling you about earlier. She said she wants to talk to me and offer her help."

"I am honored, but just how does she think she can help us?" Linda said incredulously.

"I'm not sure myself," Detective Stearns said sympathetically, "but she may have some facts about her son's murder or the events leading up to it that may help us solve your son's disappearance and, if not, then it will be another lead we can rule out."

"I see, but I doubt very seriously that she can help us. However, if you think that it is a good idea, we will agree to meet her and see what she has to say. It's just that her son died years ago and although there may be some similarities, I doubt very seriously that her child's murderer just stuck around town all this time to kidnap mine. While I'm extremely sorry for her loss, her son's killer is probably miles and miles from here or probably dead," Linda said.

Detective Stearns and Luke looked at each other as Linda finished speaking. While both agreed that the idea of a murderer still living nearby the crime after all these years seemed unrealistic, it still was a probability and worth looking into.

Detective Stearns decided to interject. "I will be going to meet with her after we say good-bye, so if she mentions anything relevant, then I will call you and we can schedule a meeting for us all in my office. If not, then at least I'll know I left no stone unturned as they say."

Linda and Luke thought that was a wise approach and told him so. Thanking him, they headed to the door, leaving Stearns alone with all his thoughts. He was glad he had opted to not show the Williamses the pictures or file material from the cold case. It was pretty obvious that Mrs. Williams had mentally shut out the idea that her son would not be found alive. Though he commended her stance and resolve, it also troubled him. Quickly straightening his office, he walked to the breakroom, poured himself a cup of coffee, and headed for the front door. As he was leaving, one of the officers called out to him that he had a phone call.

"Who is it?" he bellowed, still trying to get out of the front door without spilling his coffee.

"Some lady named Ethel," the officer yelled back. "Says she has the articles you requested and wants to know if you want them mailed or do you want to go and pick them up? She said either way it is no charge."

Stearns paused for a second trying to decide whether or not he would be able to make it there after visiting with Ms. McKenzie.

"Tell her that I'll come myself later on today and pick them up. No need to mail them." He pushed the door open again and walked toward his truck. He was actually glad that Ethel remembered him. That was another source of information that may be valuable. Hopefully Ms. McKenzie would not keep him so long so that he couldn't pick up the requested newspaper articles. It was a about a twenty to thirty-minute ride to where she resided, so he wanted to make sure he was on the road with enough time to travel back to Taylor and reach the *Taylor Tribune* before it closed. As he headed out of town, he couldn't help but stare at the park and the woods that he had only recently visited. It still looked deserted with a few cars parked near one of the entrances. He thought about pulling in but shrugged his shoulders thinking it was not that important and continued toward Ms. McKenzie's home located in Green Valley. Laurel Cove had been part of a nice subdivision years back but had now been forgotten as larger homes in more exclusive locations had been erected. Nothing fancy, mind you, but a modest group of single-story brick homes with large front yards and small back ones. Even the color of the bricks and the height of the roofs' pitch were glaring reminders of the style of a yesteryear.

Stearns scanned the mailboxes for the last name of McKenzie. After a few minutes, he located the mailbox bearing her name all the way at the very end of the cul-de-sac. He parked his car and stepped out, instinctively looking around. He wasn't really sure what to expect, figuring that McKenzie didn't really get many visitors, if any. Knocking on the door, he noticed very little movement and began to speak, "Ms. McKenzie, it's me, Detective Maris Stearns. I spoke to you on the phone earlier." Knocking louder he called her name out a few times but no answer. Walking back to his truck he heard a *clink*—the sound of deadbolts being unlocked.

"Detective?" a shrewd, petite woman said, standing directly in the doorway. "I'm Anna, please come inside and excuse the mess."

Detective Stearns followed after her, stepping here and there to avoid items on the floor as if they were small land mines. He suspected that Ms. McKenzie was a secret hoarder with all the clutter that filled up the corners of the living room. Stacks of newspapers littered most of the living area and hallway. A tattered child's blanket lay on top of an old recliner, and an outdated television set sat surrounded by other stacks of newspaper articles and a variety of trinkets. He tried not to stare too long at any of it as she ushered him toward a small, armless chair, which she cleaned off quickly and motioned for him to sit.

"Ms. McKenzie, I appreciate you seeing me, but if this is an inconvenient time for you, I can talk to you over the phone when you are ready."

Anna McKenzie looked at him seemingly oblivious to the state of her home and her surroundings. "Of course not, Detective, I called you because I want to be helpful and something tells me that I can. I know you don't understand that right now, but I assure you I believe that the monster that killed my boy, Tanner, has something to do with that other kid being taken. I know it's been years since he took my son, but I've been watching the news and it's like déjà vu, you know?"

Stearns nodded his head pretending to agree, curious about her odd comments and hoping she would elaborate further.

"I hope so, Ms. McKenzie. I have already had a conversation with Chief Roberts. He gave me some information about your son, but I would like to talk to you if you don't mind me taking notes about the events that transpired right before his disappearance. I will tell you that I have read the statement that you originally gave to the police, and though I'm sure the years have not aided your memory, I would appreciate if you would walk me through from about a week prior to his abduction."

Anna struggled to hold in her emotions as she mouthed the word "okay." She needed to be strong and open up. Detective Stearns could see her hands trembling but she continued.

"Well, that previous week we had pretty much done what we always do, you know?"

"No ma'am, I don't know. Just take your time and go day by day."

"Okay, so we stayed home like the Monday and the Tuesday. Went to the grocery store on the Wednesday and went to the park the next day. That was Thursday, then um . . . Friday. Okay, Friday he had a baseball game and the team won so I took him out to eat afterward at this restaurant up the road. Then the next day he asked me if he could go visit some of his friends who lived in the neighborhood, and I agreed. I didn't really want him to go, but my kid was a good kid, you know. Never really was into mischief or anything. He was obedient and I figured why not."

Detective Stearns looked up as he paused with his pen still in the air. "What about his father?"

"Don't get me started on that one. He left when Tanner was very young and we never saw him since. Tanner, poor thing, never gave up on him, but I did ages ago. He didn't have any communication with us since he left, so I wouldn't even know where to look for him."

"I see. No fights, threats, or reason for retaliation against your son?"

"No, no of course not. He wasn't much of a husband and father in my opinion, but he wasn't a killer. Whoever did this to my Tanner is a cold-hearted . . ."and with that she put her hand over her mouth as if to apologize for such a rash, unbridled statement.

"It's quite all right, Ms. McKenzie. I can't imagine how I would feel if I were in your place, but I'm pretty sure anger would be on my list."

Anna tried to steady her trembling hands before her emotions got any worse. If they did, she knew it would be too much of an embarrassment for the interview to continue. Detective Stearns tried not to notice, but his eyes continued to drift toward her shaking hands and her ashen skin.

Thinking quickly, he changed his line of questioning. "So, these friends of his, he had a lot? Do you know which ones he was supposed to see or visit with? Was he walking or on a bike?"

Ms. Anna looked as if she were trying desperately to answer his questions but finally looked at him apologetically. "I know it wasn't very many friends 'cause he was still shy, but I remember one of them. His name was Chip. Good kid too. Don't know or recall the others just off the top of my head, and to answer your other question, which, if I am not mistaken, you asked me already, but I can always answer again by telling you that he was only walking. He had a bike but the chain was always coming off, and I'm just not that good with mechanical things, you know."

"So, the last thing you knew was that he was walking to see his friends, and you assumed it was this kid, Chip?"

"Yes, sir."

"Did you see him actually down the street? I mean did you watch him go down the street?"

"No," Ms. McKenzie said softly. "I should have, but I didn't."

"So, did you go outside at all as he was leaving?"

Again, Ms. McKenzie replied, "No," softly.

"Were there any problems with bullies, anyone that he had offended in any way?"

"No," she said quickly and matter-of-factly, her face hard and then softening as she spoke. "Tanner was a great kid and though I would have liked for his dad to have been part of his life, I did the best I could. He wasn't a complainer and somewhat shy so I doubt very seriously he would've gotten on anybody's bad side. He was good at baseball and had friends on his team. I might've fussed at him a handful of times in his entire life, but that's about it."

"I understand," Detective Stearns said, trying to be hospitable. "So, getting back to my questions . . . When he left, he just walked right out or he lingered like he was afraid or what?"

"No, he didn't linger. He asked me and I said yes. Next thing I knew, the front door was slamming and he was outside."

"How do you know he was outside?" Detective Stearns said, looking up abruptly from his writing.

"Because he called out to me and I could tell he was outside."

"Um, okay and what did he yell out? I mean if you can recall that."

Anna McKenzie bit her lip fiercely, her fingers fidgeting again. "He said, 'Mom I'll be back soon. No worries, I'll be okay.'"

"That's it?" Detective Stearns asked.

"Yes," she said sadly. "I didn't even tell him that I loved him. You have no idea how much I regret not saying it, but I thought he was coming right back." Anna began to cry, trying to stop but unable.

Detective Stearns stretched his hand out and clasped hers. She immediately pulled it back, caught off guard by his gesture. Detective Stearns pulled his hand back as well and picked his pen up again.

"I'm sorry, Ms. McKenzie. I was trying to comfort you. You looked as if you were about to fall apart, and I was just trying to tell you that it's okay to cry and that it's not your fault."

"I know," she said a bit sarcastically. "Everyone keeps telling me that and yes, I have come to terms with the murderer of my son and that he is the one responsible. But I still have to live with the fact that it began with that first step outside and that I didn't go outside and watch him make it back safely and that, as of now, no justice has been served for my boy's death. You don't know how I feel."

Detective Stearns put his pen down and looked around. "Okay, Ms. McKenzie, but I'm not here for anything other than seeking information that may help me find the missing boy from Taylor. You wanted to talk to me so I came. I'm truly sorry for everything that has happened, but maybe there is something that we've missed. At first, I would have dismissed your son's situation as something totally unrelated to this one, but there are some similarities that have me wanting to know more. I sense your aggravation knowing that your son's murder is unsolved, and I can't blame you for the gamut of emotions you must have felt and are still feeling, but Chief Roberts also senses that this may be related somehow. Your help may be crucial not only to my case but in finding your son's murderer as well."

Anna looked up tiredly. Her life had felt like a prison for so long that she had hardly seen anything beyond her bars of avoidance and chains of regret. Was this young detective really telling her the truth? Was he willing to try to help her as well? He seemed as if he did and his eyes conveyed sincerity. Tanner was all she had been able to think about since he was taken. After that, her days only consisted of crying, collecting newspapers, and sleeping. It sometimes felt like an effort to just simply exist now. All of the stories in the papers from all over the country about children kidnapped or murdered—each article read with the hope that the murderer or kidnapper would confess to her son's murder. At first, she had been zealous as she searched for answers but soon the subscriptions were too costly for the budget and with no real hope of finding peace for Tanner, she'd finally given up. It had been too many years and though she had resolved to finally move on, she could not, at least not yet. With this recent kidnapping, as sad as it was, it had breathed a strange sense of hope back in her that Tanner's case could be solved.

"I will help you but not only for that child, but also for my Tanner."

Detective Stearns smiled, hopeful that she could. "So, how long was it before you realized something was wrong?"

Anna realized that in order for the conversation to be productive, she needed to put her emotions aside. "Well, it was about three or four hours later that I started getting worried. I remembered that I had made dinner or maybe I was just about finished and I went to look for him. He wasn't in his room, so I looked around the house and then I called for him outside, but he wasn't there. Just kept calling and calling. I finally went down the street, but everyone whose door I stopped at hadn't seen him. It was like he'd vanished into thin air. I called the cops after that and the rest . . . I'm sure you know."

"Well, I know some things but I don't know them from you. It's just a hunch, but I don't think someone just happened by chance to come down this road, although I'm not ruling out a random kidnapping."

"What do you mean?" Anna asked. "Do you think it's someone Tanner knew?"

"Not sure," Detective Stearns said quickly, "but my hunch is that it is definitely someone he saw or made contact with before."

Anna looked confused trying to think of who might have been in contact with Tanner. Besides school, church, the baseball team, and a few family members, she was drawing a blank as to who in their lives would be capable of doing something so sinister. "Detective, I know he . . . well, we came into contact with people back then on a daily basis. Everyone did. Trying to identify someone that 'saw' him is not enough. Chief Roberts interviewed just about everybody of interest in this town and he ruled them all out. He ended up telling me that even after they found my poor son, they still didn't have enough evidence to convict anyone. How is that possible?"

Stearns felt a bit uncomfortable but knew she deserved a response so he obliged. "Well, actually sometimes if someone is very careful, they will protect themselves from leaving DNA, like hair, by wearing gloves, hats, or anything that might keep them covered. There is also the issue regarding a lack of evidence on a decomposing body . . . I mean 'person' once he or she is found. The longer it takes to find the person the less likely any evidence is preserved. Basically, the sooner found, the better law enforcement's chance in securing what is needed in tracking down an individual who would do such a heinous crime."

"I think I understand," Anna said, feeling appreciative for Detective Stearns' response. She wondered if he had been around when Tanner had disappeared if he would have been able to make any difference. Though he was young, he was a quick thinker with a keen eye. The more she spoke to him the more comfortable she felt. She had not felt comfortable with ANYONE in a very long time.

"Well, perhaps someone did 'see' him and followed y'all home not long before Tanner was taken. Do you recall Chief Roberts asking anyone about strange vehicles seen in the neighborhood?"

"Oh, I wouldn't know. I know he asked me if I had seen anything strange the day Tanner was abducted, but I don't recall him asking about before Tanner was taken, but it's been a while. So you could probably ask him yourself. I'm sure he would tell ya."

"I will be sure to ask him, Ms. McKenzie."

"You are welcome to check his room if you like also. I've kept it just the way it was, so I only ask that you not change anything. I . . . I would be upset if you did because it's all I have left of him, you know."

Stearns nodded. "Of course, ma'am. I still have a few more questions to ask you, but after that we can go take a look together."

Anna was pleased with that response. "Oh, I'm sorry, I thought I had answered them all."

"That's okay," Stearns said, "sometimes I pause in my questioning, which makes people think that. I'm sorry if it appeared like I was done. I did have a few errands still to run today, but those need to wait until we finish. I want to hear about the night before. You know the one that you say you both went to a restaurant after Tanner had won his baseball game."

"There's really not much to tell," Anna said, beginning slowly. We went to his game—"

"Okay let me interrupt you there. Where was the game held?"

"It was at the sports complex in town. There is only one."

"Okay," Detective Stearns said, writing something down again and circling it. "And what time was that? It's okay to not remember the exact time that day—I know that's been years ago—but an approximate will do."

"Okay, well I'd have to say it was probably about 6ish. His games usually started about 7 p.m. and we arrived there early so they could warm up first."

"Were there a lot of people?"

"Yes," Anna said. "It was their championship game. The sports complex was packed and even the local news stations were out there filming everyone on the team after they had won. I remember Tanner being so shy in front of the camera, but I was so proud . . . so very proud of him."

Detective Stearns smiled sincerely, seeing her face light up as she talked about such a precious moment for her son. Her worn face looked like she hadn't smiled like that in a very long time.

"Then what? Did anyone get near him, accost him at any time?"

"No, I don't think so. I mean I wasn't with him at all times because the coach talked to them after the game, and they all went together to the concession stand a couple of times. But I was with him or watching him the rest of the time, and I didn't see anything or anyone. The more I think about it, I'm pretty sure that Chief Roberts questioned me about all of that years ago."

"I understand, Ms. McKenzie, but I'm needing this information again for my own file, and I appreciate your patience answering these questions."

Anna nodded.

"What about afterward? Where did you go next?"

"Well, Tanner and I got in the car and, since he was hungry, I took him to Lynn's Restaurant to celebrate. It was a little expensive for my budget, but he had done so good I wanted to splurge. We ate and then we left and went home. Well, wait . . . there was something but it's not that important."

"What, what is it, Ms. McKenzie? Please let me decide if it's important or not."

Anna continued. "Well, there was a young guy who was at the restaurant, like a dishwasher or something. He was a good-looking fellow who gave Tanner a high-five and a peppermint. I thought he was just being kind, so I didn't make anything of it. People in Southern towns are just nice like that, ya know."

7

Detective Stearns said nothing at first as he continued to write more onto his ever-growing stack of notes. But this peculiar comment sounded promising.

"So, this guy . . . he just came up to you or to Tanner?"

Anna paused, thinking for a moment. "It was just to Tanner, I think. I don't really remember him ever speaking to me. Besides, we got to the restaurant late, and I think the workers were probably just trying to get us out the door so they could leave too."

Stearns nodded, pretending to agree with her but deep down his gut did not. *Why would someone like a dishwasher come out and speak with Tanner?*

"Detective, he was at the table cleaning it off when we showed up. When he congratulated Tanner about the game, I honestly did not think anything of it. There were so many people, as I told you before, at their championship game that I guess I figured he was just another local who was proud of our team."

"Did he happen to linger or anything?"

"Linger?"

"Yeah, you know, try to keep coming back to the table, watching you both?"

"No, at least I don't think so, and I'm pretty sure if he had lingered, I would have said something. As I said earlier, Tanner and I had been by ourselves for quite a while and had gotten used to it. I don't have a habit of just letting ANYONE in."

Anna stared at Detective Stearns as she spoke hoping that he would understand that she desperately needed someone to confide in. Someone she could trust now that Tanner was gone.

"I know you and your son had a very special bond," Stearns said, sensing that she needed encouragement to continue. "Did he approach you or Tanner at all after the meal?"

"Well, when we left the table, I believe he had come back from out of the kitchen to clean off the table."

"Any interaction?"

"No."

"What was Tanner doing?"

"He went to use the restroom while I paid the tab at the counter."

"Did you see anyone else go in the bathroom with him?"

"I don't recall but it was a public restroom, you know, like with more than one stall."

"Oh, okay, but did you see the dishwasher or anyone else head toward the bathroom?"

"I had my back turned while I paid the lady our tab. There might have been, but my back wasn't turned for long."

"Then what?"

"Well, Tanner had walked back to where I was standing and we walked out of the restaurant, got in the car, and went home."

"Did he mention anything to you on the way home?"

"No, not really. I wish I remembered every word but I really can't. Pretty sure most of it was about the game though. He really did like playing sports . . . I miss him so much." Anna put her head down as she brought her hands to her face. She knew now was not the time, but thinking of Tanner and what happened always brought her to tears.

Detective Stearns watched with sympathy but there wasn't much he could do. Looking down at his watch, he glanced at the time realizing that if he was going to go by the *Taylor Tribune* he'd better get a move on it. "Ms. McKenzie, I am going to be leaving soon. But . . . I would like to see Tanner's room . . . that is, if you feel like showing me still."

Anna nodded and got up from her seat, brushing away strands of hair and tears. She steered her way slowly through the stacks of papers and down the hallway where one door was shut and gently opened it. It smelled stale and Detective Stearns turned his head away quickly, the odor repugnant to him.

"Sorry," Anna said. "I told you that I had left his room just the way it was the day he left. I used to come in here constantly after, well, after he was taken, but now I don't go in it often. So, I'm sure it's a bit dusty in there."

Detective Stearns said nothing as he tried to take a few gulps of air before entering the room. As expected, it was a typical boy's room with posters hung haphazardly and the theme of a popular superhero both on the wall art and in random toys scattered about. A matching pillow and comforter lay neatly across a twin bed with a small, wooden headboard that had pieces of stickers left on it from when they had been torn off in too much of a hurry. A baseball bat with a tattered glove was propped near a matching dresser with a few pictures of the little boy and his mother positioned atop of it. However, a small pile of clothes caught his eye, and he walked further into the room and bent down.

"These clothes . . . tell me, have they been here since Tanner was taken?"

"Yes, why?" Anna asked confused.

"There is a baseball outfit in this pile. Is this by chance the one he wore the night before he disappeared?"

"I'd have to see, it's been so long, but I would think. I mean, he only had one uniform. He had a habit of leaving his dirty clothes in a pile for me to pick up when I did the laundry. Because it was only him and me in the house I didn't do the laundry as much as I probably should've. After I buried him, I refused to move any of his things, choosing to leave them just as he had left them. Guess they smell, huh?"

"It's not the smell, Ms. McKenzie; I am going to ask you for a very big favor."

"And what is that, Detective?"

"I would like to have these clothes, the baseball uniform in particular, analyzed. Did anyone ask you for this before, like Chief Roberts maybe?"

"Nope, no one did. Chief Roberts only asked me what he was wearing at the time he left the house and then when he was found, he told me that they had kept his clothes as evidence and that they wouldn't be returned to me." Anna looked as if she was about to cry again but held her composure. "If you promise you will not damage them and bring them back to me the same then yes, you can." She bent down to pick them up and Detective Stearns grabbed her hand quickly. Anna looked up, taken aback by his response.

"I need to put on some gloves and remove them myself, Ms. McKenzie. I have a bag and gloves in the car. I don't want our fingertips or anything else on these clothes until after they have been thoroughly tested. Be right back."

Stearns jumped up and made his way quickly down the hall, through the living room, and out the front door. His vehicle was still unlocked so he opened his passenger door and then the glove box. In it was a small box that he pulled out and returned quickly into Ms. McKenzie's home. Opening it up near the clothes, he eased his hands into the latex gloves and slid the clothes one at a time slowly into small, separate plastic bags, taking extra precautionary steps for the baseball uniform itself. Then he pulled the latex gloves off, put them back in the box, and tied each of the bags closed.

"Thank you, Ms. McKenzie, I promise to return all the items to you," Detective Stearns said, collecting the bags in his hands as he stood back up.

"I'm not sure what you think you'll be able to find by taking them, but please let me know. I want Tanner's killer caught, and if he is somehow responsible for the other boy's disappearance, then I hope he is caught before he hurts another innocent child."

"Of course, Ms. McKenzie." Stearns glanced at his watch again and said his farewells.

He mused as he drove away thinking to himself. The discovery of these items was a new lead, and though the Williamses might have some misgivings about his approach, something told him that he was close to uncovering an important breakthrough in the case. He still needed to pick up the documents he had requested from the local newspaper and contact Mr. and Mrs. Williams about his meeting with Ms. McKenzie. A phone call to the chief was also something that needed to be done sooner than later. Yawning, he drove until he saw the familiar sign: *Taylor Tribune*.

Ethel was there still waiting for his arrival and Detective Stearns smiled apologetically but gratefully as he opened the glass door. A short, rather large lady greeted him with horn-rimmed glasses and rosy cheeks. "Detective Stearns, I'm Ethel, we spoke on the phone."

"Yes, Mrs. Ethel," Stearns said, extending a firm handshake. Ethel shook it and jovially motioned for him to follow her through a long corridor and into a small office located toward the back of the building. *Taylor Tribune* had been around ever since Detective Stearns could recall, maybe even before his grandparents' time. It had always been owned and operated by family until recently when it was bought out by a larger syndicated newspaper that covered a regional area, much bigger than Taylor. Mrs. Ethel had stayed on to help ease everyone, both new and old, into a peaceful transition, or at the very least was trying to. Though a few things had remained the same, there was enough "big city talk" suggesting that the entire staff would be laid off with the thinking that fresh faces with negotiable salaries was the step forward for the in-debt newspaper.

Ethel had agreed that changes had been necessary for the survival of the company. However, as longtime friends and coworkers began to slowly be released with very little notice, she started to worry about the integrity of this company and her own employment security. Living in Taylor all her life and working for the local newspaper for so many years, she had become acquainted with many of the residents and their children, as well. She truly cared about her job, and writing about the locals and their accomplishments brought her enjoyment.

"Here ya go, Detective, I got your package right here," Ethel said, eyeing the young detective.

"Thank you, Mrs. Ethel!" he said as he took the manila envelope from her hands.

"I made copies of everything we had in the archives that you asked me for, and I definitely had to do some digging," Ethel said proudly.

"I appreciate that, Mrs. Ethel, I really do."

"That boy still missing, huh?"

"Yes, ma'am, I'm sorry to report that we are still trying to locate him."

"Any leads?"

"Maybe, but I'm really not at liberty to disclose it."

"Why, 'cause I'm the 'media'?" she said a bit sarcastically, poking at him.

"No, Mrs. Ethel, now you know I can't always disclose everything to you and that is because we have to stay ahead of the kidnapper. We can't have whoever it is knowing our every move."

Ethel looked up, her ego sufficiently stroked. Detective Stearns smiled. Ethel was a kind lady but he had heard from others in his office that she was just a wee bit sensitive. *Guess they were right*, he thought, still smiling.

"Do I owe you anything, Mrs. Ethel?"

"'Course not," she said, batting her eyes. "Just let me know when I can print that you found that missing boy."

He smiled and began walking down the corridor and out of the doors toward his vehicle. The package seemed light, but he was anxious to get both that and the clothes of the deceased boy back to the department.

"You back for the rest of the day, Stearns?" a voice called as he entered his office. Glancing back he saw Chief Roberts propping his rotund body against the wall and wiping the beads of sweat that had formed across his large forehead with a small handkerchief.

"Chief . . . surprised to see you here."

"Well, don't be," Chief Bear Paw said with a heave. "I'm here to help as I told you. We need to put our resources together to find this boy. They told me you are trying to organize a search party, as I had suggested, in the wooded area beginning tomorrow morning. I'd like to aid you in your endeavors. Because I have gone through this, my experience might be helpful to you and earn a little recognition for myself."

Stearns wasn't about to turn down any law enforcement agencies in the continued search for Aidan Williams, just as long as they didn't try to do anything willy-nilly or usurp his authority.

"Sounds good to me, Chief. We could use the manpower, for sure." Anything more?"

"More, what?" Stearns asked, looking at Chief Roberts.

"Got any closer in bringing this perp to justice?"

"As a matter of fact, I got a phone call from Ms. Anne McKenzie, you know that old case you told me about?"

The chief looked at him squarely "Yes, but I don't see as how she could provide much help. They say she's a basket case now, and, besides, her son's death was years ago."

"I know that, Chief. There are papers stacked everywhere and she looked frail and very unkempt. I actually went to her house, so I speak from experience. However, she is not a basket case. She just needs closure."

Chief Roberts nodded, still looking perplexed. "So why did she call you?"

"She thought she could help. I guess she figured with the Williams' kid missing that maybe there was something she could do."

"Humph," Chief Roberts said in disbelief.

"You scoff, Chief, but actually I think she might have given me something useful."

"And what is that?" Chief Roberts said incredulously.

"The night of the baseball game, she and her son went out to eat. She told me that there was a young man who had some contact with

Tanner. Since she hadn't removed the clothes he wore that night from his room, I thought I'd bring them in for analysis."

"For what? That case has been closed for years."

"You were the one who told me to go look in the woods near Green Valley. You told me about the old case."

"Yes, but only because I thought there were some similarities and because we had found the young boy there. So if you hadn't yet looked there, then I felt you should. Not for you to get caught up on an old cold case while trying to resolve your own investigation. What are you thinking? Pretty sure that creep is long gone."

"I know you are gonna think this is crazy, but my gut tells me somehow, someway these kidnappings are related."

"Well, that is something I'd expect from a rookie, but you've been here for quite a while, Detective. You have enough experience to know that anyone capable of this heinous crime may have stayed a while afterward. But there is a little different makeup to these types of individuals than, let's say, an arsonist who wants to admire his handiwork. This kind of person is probably sitting in another country, far away from places like this that are small and friendly and have good law enforcement." He chuckled as he spoke, looking around the department for nods of approval.

Detective Stearns paused, deciding it best to choose his words carefully "Chief, I just have a feeling that these kidnappings with boys close to the same age, both involved in sports and in towns mere miles from one another is more than a coincidence."

"Do you honestly have any idea how many boys and girls are kidnapped daily with at least two or three similarities? Please don't waste the Williams' time by searching up a tree that there is nothing in."

"Chief, begging your pardon, I'm not trying to waste anyone's time, especially the Williams'." Detective Stearns paused, realizing that his voice had been loud enough for others to stop and take notice. A few officers had stopped walking entirely, purposefully lingering to hear their raised voices. Choosing a different approach he continued, "I know you are an excellent police chief and I hope you continue to be, but I've a hunch that just won't let up and since Tanner's killer was never found or prosecuted, he may have been emboldened to stay here and not leave."

"Okay, for the sake of argument," Chief Roberts said, sounding exacerbated, "let's say you are correct. If this guy were to be the same one who took that other kid, then you are already too late. I think you need to review that file that I gave you and take a good look again at those pictures. You had better hope it's not the same guy or you are gonna have one awful conversation with the parents."

Stearns nodded. "I'll talk to you in a few." He grabbed the items in his hand and walked quickly to the lab, choosing to avoid an obvious unnecessary debate with Chief Roberts.

"Sarah," Stearns called out as he knocked gently on the open door to announce his presence.

"Maris!" Sarah said, looking up happily. Stearns smiled. Sarah was one of his favorites at the department, having attended the same high school in their younger days. Bright, sharp, witty . . . she was a good friend; they had worked together for over three years.

"I need a tremendous favor, Sarah."

"Okay. I hate to be the one to tell you this, but anybody who brings something here to be analyzed asks for a 'tremendous favor' because a case depends on it."

"I know, just this is involving the missing kid." He put the bag of clothes onto the countertop.

"Of course, I can put a rush on it . . . those are his clothes?"

"Not exactly," Stearns said, watching Sarah's hand recoil back from the bag.

"They do belong to a child though, but one that passed away years ago."

"Oh, poor thing," Sarah said with sympathy.

"I know, it is tragic, but right now I need you to run some tests on these particular clothes because they may have some bearing on the new kidnapping."

"You got it, Maris. I'll take a look at them now and let you know what I find. It may take a little time though."

"How much time?" Stearns asked, trying to convey the urgency.

"A couple of days?" Sarah said, looking back at him. "It's complicated, you know that. I got a few tests that have to be run, and that could take some time to do and there is the issue of a report."

"Sarah, I don't have that kinda time . . . this boy, Aidan . . . does not have that kinda time."

Sarah looked at Detective Stearns. He looked like he had actually aged since last week. She knew the stress was getting to him, and she wished there was something she could do or say to let him know it would be okay, but there wasn't and at the very least it might come across as disingenuous.

"I promise to do what I can."

"I know, Sarah . . . please come get me as soon as you do." Stearns walked back toward his office and opened the door, quickly closing it behind him.

Once inside he pulled out the file on Tanner McKenzie from the inside of the desk drawer and set it next to the package from Ethel. He knew that the Williamses would need another update, so he opened up the envelope and pulled out the small handful of newspaper articles. He put each one side by side, instantly recognizing one of the articles with a picture of Tanner in his baseball uniform standing amongst other children also dressed in theirs and all of them smiling proudly. Stearns couldn't help but feel a lump in his throat. Even if he had seen horrific things, crimes against children were the worst. Not that any other crime was excusable, but for some reason ones specifically directed toward children just seemed incorrigible.

There were a few other photos of the baseball team as they had won their way to the championship. The rest dealt with the disappearance, the search, and, of course, the grizzly details of his murder. Detective Stearns began reading through them one by one, making notes as he went. A picture of Tanner's mother caught him by surprise. She was distraught, of course, but her features were striking. She had been a very pretty lady, now nothing more than a shell, reduced to a broken, angry woman. The articles were somewhat vague about the search, which he was afraid of, but it was protocol. However, he was hoping to glean whether or not there was anything that might reveal a pattern to be deciphered.

After a while, he put his head down and rubbed his eyes. Nothing was popping out at him, and as much as he had tried to not let this case get to him, it already had. It angered him to not be able to pursue any serious leads about the Williams' son, but the worst part was that he had nothing to tell them. Before long, Stearns had actually begun to sleep, thoroughly exhausted.

"Maris, Maris Stearns! Are you in there?" a voice yelled out.

8

Detective Stearns jolted out of his seat.

"I'm here," he said, opening the door. It was Sarah. "What is it? What did you find?" he could tell from her expression that she had uncovered something, and his heart raced with anticipation.

"Maris, I'm sorry that I woke you up, but your orders were to come and get you as soon as I found something."

Stearns nodded, "Go on."

"Okay," Sarah said, "follow me down to the lab."

Stearns followed after Sarah, glancing at the clock in the hallway. It was already night and he felt a twinge of guilt at having to make Sarah work so quickly. But perhaps this hunch of his was going to pay off.

Once inside, Sarah closed the door behind them and motioned for him to sit on one of the stools nearest the counter where he had originally brought the plastic bag containing Tanner's clothes.

"Okay," Sarah said, sounding serious, "let's get started. The first analysis that I conducted was for any traces of chemicals and/or anything that would cause me to be concerned. What I found was grass, soil, and alkylbenzene sulfonates. Basically, laundry detergent. No real reason to be suspicious. Next, I uncovered a few small strands of hair approximately two inches in length, one a lighter color, the other a couple of shades darker. These hairs were found on the baseball shirt but not on the pants. I next examined the few clothing items that remained and found another couple of the lighter shades of hair as well as a long strand, which was also darker. I checked them all separately for patterns and pigment and concluded that the lighter strands of hair were from the same individual, and both the long strand and the other darker shade of hair belonged to another group of people, two other people to be exact." Stearns knew that Tanner was light-haired so more likely than not, it was Tanner's own hair. But the other two, he wasn't so sure. Perhaps the longer strand was Ms. Anna's, which would leave one type of hair unaccounted for.

"Can you tell me anything about the darker hairs found?"

"Well, yes. Let me back up a few steps. One, they are all human and all from Caucasians, as you can see here on the microscope." Sarah pointed to the computer screen where a long cylinder-shaped object appeared. "The hairs are coded in the cross section and the pigment is more evenly distributed from the root up."

Stearns nodded, letting her continue.

"So we can also see that through the comparison microscope, the lighter hairs have not really lost any pigment and have a cut tip, which leads me to believe that those belong to a child and not an adult. They also would be coming from the head region due to the appearance of the cut tip, which is what hair would look like after a haircut under the microscope." Sarah pushed a couple of keys, showing another image of a cylinder with a variety of different ends.

"Okay, I think then that we can deduce that the blondish hairs belonged to the boy?" Stearns asked, looking at Sarah.

"Well, these strands are old as are the others, so I would still need some elimination samples from any next of kin or other family members and then perhaps from a hairbrush or something similar of the young boy's. It would help for sure in my research."

"I think I can accommodate you. These clothes were given to me by the deceased boy's mother, so I'm sure she would be cooperative. But you got me curious about the other darker strands. They're not from a child are they?"

"You are correct. Both the long and the darker short hairs collected show evidence of pigment loss, which in my line of work is indicative of age. As we age, we begin to lose some of the pigment in our hair follicles, making it easier to decipher a few things as they fall out, which happens on a daily basis in the telegenic phase."

"Whoa, Sarah, you're talking over my head now," Detective Stearns said, chuckling.

"It's all right, most people really don't think about how much hair actually falls out each day, and that's just from the head region."

"Yuck!" Stearns said.

"It's not yuck; it's just our bodies' genetic makeup. With the long strand of hair, I would most likely determine this to be a female hair."

"Because of the length?" Stearns asked, quickly trying to be helpful.

"Well, although that is a factor, since guys are starting to wear their hair much longer, it wasn't that reason I based my, shall we say, informal conclusion."

"What then?"

"Well, I've seen my share of female and male hair samples that typically have been altered in some way like dyeing or coloring or things such as styling products, curling irons, or straightening ones. This causes changes to the follicle over time, and under a microscope on the long strand it appeared that some of those had occurred. It is my opinion that the longer strand is indeed female. So, if you are looking for a male killer or kidnapper, I would say the only other remaining hair is your best bet."

"Would you conclude that it is from a male?" Stearns asked.

Sarah once again pressed against the keys and moved her cursor toward another image. "Yes, I would. The pigment and shape is suggestive of the head region again but of an adult male."

"The pigment loss, is it a lot? Can you determine age?"

"The age, mind you, would only be an approximate," Sarah retorted, "but it would most likely be a young male maybe early twenties. There is pigment loss but not that much. It is definitely a secondary transfer to the boy, but whoever he was, he wasn't around the child for too long, at least not while he was wearing the uniform. Since there is only the one strand, I would have to say that this was a random encounter, not someone who spent a lengthy time with the child, like say an immediate family member. I hope this was helpful, but I will still need for you to gather samples from the mother, father, et cetera."

"There wasn't a male figure in the home," Stearns replied, "just the boy and the mother. Think the father had split some time ago and did not have any interaction with the child."

Sarah nodded. "I understand; just get me what you can, so I can finalize something to put in the file. In the meantime, I'll send this sample over to the guys to see if we have anything in the database that matches this hair sample. It's a long shot but anything is possible."

"Thanks," Stearns said. "I'll make a few phone calls to get you what I need on my end." Stearns left.

Back in his office, Stearns grabbed the phone and dialed the number for Anna McKenzie. It rang a few times and then he heard someone pick up.

"Hello," Anna's voice sounded like a whisper.

"It's Detective Stearns, ma'am. I know it's late, Ms. McKenzie, but I needed to know if you would be agreeable to bringing in a few items to the police department for additional analysis." Stearns wanted to tell her that they had found an unknown male hair but refrained. If it turned out to be nothing, he didn't want her getting her hopes up after all these years, only to be disappointed once again that her child's killer still remained at large.

"We needed to gather some samples of your son's hair and yours. Say like from a hairbrush or something like that."

"What's all this for?" Anna asked, trying to understand why her hair was necessary.

Detective Stearns tried to explain as best as he could about ruling out the hair of Tanner and identifying any others that were present, carefully avoiding discussion of what Sarah had discovered so far.

"I'm not sure where the Taylor Police Department is located," Anna said after he had finished.

"That's okay, Ms. McKenzie," Stearns said. He gave her the directions to the department. He was pretty sure that she had not driven or gotten out of the house much since her son's death and inwardly commended her strength for trying to do what she could to aid in the investigation, even if it also benefited her own interests of discovering the man who took her son from her.

"It's been a while since I've been to Taylor, I appreciate the directions. Can I come in the morning?"

"Forgive me, but if you could bring it over this evening, I'd appreciate it."

"I was just about to call it a night and head to bed, but if it's that important to you, I can leave in a few minutes and head that way."

"Yes, Ms. McKenzie that would be perfect. Once you arrive, ask for me and they will direct you straight to my office where we can talk."

"Okay," Anna said, hanging up the phone. She was hesitant about leaving the house and driving there to see Detective Stearns, but she knew it was necessary and that she would have to muster the will to go. Pulling her robe off and grabbing a pair of jeans and a blouse, she quickly dressed and noticed her hairbrush on the dresser. She grabbed it and walked down the hall to Tanner's room. His brush was near his nightstand and she reached out slowly to take it, not sure if she was emotionally ready to part with it.

"Let him go," Anna mumbled to herself, but the advice sounded hollow. She forced herself to grab the small brush quickly, afraid that if she didn't hurry she may change her mind. An empty plastic grocery bag in the kitchen was a perfect holder, so she shoved them both in there and grabbed her car keys. Anna's hands shook as she sat behind the wheel. *What's wrong with me?* she thought, not really sure why her nerves were still going haywire. Although she very seldom drove ever since Tanner's death, she still did on occasion, but it was indeed a struggle to will herself out of the house. She did not feel the waves of anxiety before like she was experiencing now. She closed her eyes tightly and steadied her hands. "You can do this, you can do this . . . YOU CAN DO THIS . . ." Anna opened her eyes quickly and shoved the key into the ignition, turning them forward and hearing the rumble of the motor.

Thirty minutes later, she arrived at the Taylor Police Department. She turned the car off and grabbed the keys along with the grocery bag and headed toward the entrance.

"May I speak to Mr. Stearns?" she asked as a female officer passed her by.

"Detective Maris Stearns?"

"Yes ma'am, he is expecting me."

"Uh, okay. Right this way." Anna followed the officer as she walked through a maze of offices, finally arriving at one that had Detective Stearns' name written on the frosted glass partition in the middle of the door.

"Thanks," Anna said, looking at the officer.

As the officer smiled and walked away, Anna knocked on the door softly. Detective Stearns opened it and ushered her inside. It was warm and nicely decorated, instantly making Anna feel a little more at ease.

"I brought what you asked for, Detective," Anna said, setting the plastic bag on his desk.

Stearns replied, "Thank you, let's see what you have here."

Anna fumbled with the top of the plastic bag, exposing the two hairbrushes.

"That's perfect, Ms. McKenzie." Stearns watched as Anna's eyes appeared watery. "I know this must be hard for you, but just like the clothes, they will be returned to you shortly. I'm just taking these items to the lab, okay?"

Anna nodded, assuring him she would remain in her seat.

Stearns scurried down to the lab where Sarah had her eye pressed against one of the microscopes. "Sarah, I've got the items you wanted."

"Thanks. Please just set them down on the counter near the clothes you brought in earlier."

"Okay," Stearns said as he sat the bag down and headed for the door.

"You know what's odd?" Stearns turned around, hearing Sarah's voice.

"No, what?"

"The long strand . . . I did some more analysis and it appears the female it belongs to was on some serious medication. Even worse, I actually found traces of amphetamines. How old did you say this boy's mother was? And did anyone mention her having a drug problem?"

Stearns swallowed hard. Ms. McKenzie didn't look like the type at all, and she couldn't be older than early thirties.

"No, I've met Ms. McKenzie. Doesn't seem like the type to do drugs like what you are implying. I didn't ask her age, but since I've seen her and spoken to her, I wouldn't put her age more than 35."

Sarah frowned, eyebrows furrowing. "Well, then it's not her."

"What do you mean it's not her?"

"Stearns, I'm going to compare what you just brought me, but if I didn't know any better I'd say this long strand belonged to another female, but definitely older. Maybe I should have the guys also run this strand in the database?"

"Absolutely," Stearns said, "and tell them this is a priority."

Sarah stuck her thumb up in the air and put her eye back on the microscope. Detective Stearns walked back to his office as he struggled with his thoughts. *What was the other strand doing on his clothes? Does it belong to some other female at the baseball park? Is Ms. McKenzie telling me the truth?* His mind raced with how to approach the subject with her. Perhaps he should wait until Sarah had examined both the hairbrushes just to be sure. Stearns walked back into his office where Ms. McKenzie had patiently waited.

"Everything okay?" Anna asked, reading the concern on his face.

"Everything's good. They need to analyze the clothes and hairbrushes and get back to me as soon as they can."

"How long does that normally take?"

"Depends. Right now the lab is not that busy, and they have agreed to put a rush on anything that might have some bearing on the Williams' child."

"Oh, I hope so," Anna said, sounding sad.

"I do too; we just need to be patient."

"Patient?" Anna said sarcastically. "I know it's not your fault, but I've been patient for years."

"I am sorry for your loss like I've told you before, but I cannot speed things up any faster than I am. Believe me, I've tried. I've been assured that everything is being done in a timely manner. As soon as I know something, I will let you know as well."

Anna bit her lip. She knew she was wrong to be so bitter. It wasn't going to fix anything and it definitely wasn't going to win over anyone.

"Have the Williamses been notified of me being here?"

"Notified?" Stearns asked confused. "No, no one was notified. Should they be?"

"I'm not sure, just thought that it would be nice to meet them."

"I'm not sure they want to meet anyone right now, Ms. McKenzie. They've just had their child kidnapped, just as you did. Not to be rude, but what makes you think that they would want that. Did you?"

"I don't recall just what I wanted back then besides my son back. I understand what you're saying, but I figured that maybe I could be helpful."

"You already have been, Ms. Anna." Stearns' voice became softer. "There's nothing more that you need to do."

"But what if you run all those so-called tests on everything and it's just a bunch of his hair or mine and all of this was pointless and a waste of all our time?"

"What if it is? At the very least you will have known that we tried."

"You are right and I am grateful. I'm unhappy, as you can tell, and I'm barking at others for no reason. I really shouldn't have gotten snappy earlier."

"It's okay, I think I got a little of that at your house as well, but I've seen much worse."

Stearns paused unsure of how long it would take Sarah to run the additional testing. He was hoping that she would finish and call for him before the evening was out.

"I'd like to ask you again about the man at the restaurant."

"The dishwashing guy?"

"Yeah, him. I was going over my notes, and I realized that I had not asked you more about the restaurant you had gone to."

"Oh, it was Lynn's. Nice place."

"Did you ever go back?"

"No, after Tanner was taken, I didn't get out too much after that. I mean, I go pay bills, grocery shop, and have my oil changed. But I haven't been out to a restaurant since that night. It just hurt too badly."

"Do you think you could recall his face if I asked the sketch artist to come in and speak with you?"

"I doubt it, Detective. I've spent years in my mental prison but only with the thoughts of my son on my mind. Not the guy at the restaurant. I mean, not to sound mean, but he was a random guy who complimented my son on the game. I didn't make it a point to remember his name tag if he had one nor do I really remember his face. Perhaps if I saw him in a lineup, then I might be able to identify him. Other than that, I can't offer any assistance."

Stearns expected as much but it was worth a try. "That's okay; it's been a while back. But like all things, sometimes if you focus on them, it may jog your memory. You can always call me if you think of something later that you may feel is important."

"I will, Detective. Now if you will excuse me, it's getting a little late and I don't see as well at night as I used to. My eye doctor says I should wear glasses, but I think it would just make me feel even older. So—" Anna McKenzie stopped as Sarah poked her head in the office, lightly tapping on the door as she did.

9

"Stearns, do you have a minute?"

"Sure, Ms. McKenzie was just leaving."

"I can wait if you need me to," Anna said, quickly sensing something was important.

"Okay," Stearns said, quickly following Sarah out of his office and back toward the lab.

"What's up?" Stearns asked as soon as they were out of earshot.

"Something, you are NEVER gonna believe."

"What? The suspense is killing me." Stearns hated surprises.

"Remember that long strand you thought was the mother's hair?"

"Yes," Stearns said slowly.

"Well, it belongs to a woman miles from here, and she came up because she is in the database as deceased from a drug overdose."

"What? Say that again?" Stearns couldn't believe what he was hearing.

"I know," Sarah said, speaking again a bit out of breath, "as crazy as this seems, I ran the strand multiple times, compared it to the hairbrush of the mother, Anna McKenzie, and ran it down to be analyzed further in the database to see if we would have a match. Looks like the DNA is a perfect match for a lady who died the same year as that young boy, Tanner McKenzie. How in the world could that woman's hair be on his baseball uniform if she was already deceased?"

"Ask one of the officers to get me all the next of kin and anyone who might have lived with her or been in close proximity to her."

"Sure thing," Sarah said.

"What about the other darker-colored hair? Have you found anything yet on that one?"

"Nope, nothing further. But I've got the guys working on it, I promise."

"Good," Stearns said. "In the meantime, I need to make a few phone calls and tell Ms. McKenzie to go on home."

Stearns felt awful as he thought about the family of Aidan Williams, sitting at their home pensively waiting for something, anything. Numerous volunteers had already called in to the station for the search, and he had welcomed every one of them. As scheduled, it would begin at first light and he needed to be out there as well to help head the ever-growing band of supporters. Hopefully, the Williamses were aware of how many had either shown up or called in since the kidnapping. The overwhelming show of support was one thing Detective Stearns was pleased about. He felt bad at having left Ms. McKenzie waiting for him in his office, but he had little other option.

The door was still open from when he had walked out before, and Ms. McKenzie sat in the same seat appearing unmoved but looking rather surprised to see him back so soon.

"I thought you'd be a while."

"Nope, back already. That was Sarah. She found a few hairs on Tanner's baseball uniform and was perplexed to find a long strand from a deceased woman."

"Deceased woman?" Anna shot back in dismay.

"That's what I said, but she is certain of it. That's why we asked for the hairbrushes, which you so graciously brought by my office. I originally assumed the long strand was your hair, but after comparing the hair samples, it does not match yours."

"Well, what does this mean now?"

"It's very complicated, Ms. McKenzie, and I really don't have the time or all of the information to answer your questions right now, but we are searching for anyone who may have known her and can give us a better understanding of why her hair was on your son's clothing."

"How long will it all take?"

"I have no idea. I know you are just as excited about this recent discovery as I am, but there could be many reasons for it being there that may or may not affect any investigation, new or old. I told you that I would keep you apprised of any new developments and indeed I have. Please, there is nothing more you can do and, as you said yourself, you do not drive too well at night."

Anna nodded knowing that she was being excused and resolved to simply return to her home and wait. After she had said good-bye, Stearns pulled out the phone book out and located the phone number to Lynn's Restaurant in Green Valley. He glanced at his watch, noticing that the hours of operation in the ad indicated they were about to close.

He quickly dialed the number and a polite voice answered. "Lynn's Restaurant, how may I help you?"

"Hi, may I please speak with the owner of your establishment?"

"Was something wrong with your food, sir? Do you need to make a complaint?"

Stearns chuckled, "No ma'am. This is Detective Maris Stearns with the Taylor Police Department."

"What happened?" the female voice asked, sounding concerned.

"Nothing ma'am, I simply needed to ask him a few questions about an old employee."

"Oh, okay," she said cheerfully, glad to hear it wasn't an emergency. "Hold for just a minute, I'll go get him."

Detective Stearns waited patiently until he heard the sound of a gruff male voice clear his throat and speak into the phone. "Yes, this is the owner."

"Good, this is Detective Stearns."

"A detective? What's this all about?"

"Don't be alarmed; it's nothing you've done, I assure you."

"Well, then I don't understand."

"That's okay. Let me explain," Detective Stearns said slowly. "Do you keep logs or personnel files on everyone you hire?"

"If it's not too far back, why?"

"I'm trying to find out who all was employed by you from ten years back to current. Is that possible?"

"Oh, I would have to talk to my lawyer about that. Those records have social security numbers and things like that. I don't know that I can just hand them over. What is all that for anyway?"

"We are conducting an investigation regarding a kidnapping in Taylor and have reason to suspect that an old kidnapping case may be related. We could use your help in this investigation. Particularly I am looking for someone who may have been hired to clean dishes during that time period. I have no problem with you blotting out sensitive information. I'd hate to call the judge up and ask him to prepare an order allowing me to search your premises and any documents I may feel are relevant for such a simple request."

"Hold on a minute, let me see what I can do . . . and even if I have records that far back."

"Great, I'll hold," Detective Stearns said, hoping that he would be able to locate the documents and agree to produce them. It seemed like it was taking a while so Stearns decided to put the phone on speaker so that he wouldn't have the receiver pressed to his ear for too long. Finally, he could hear voices muffled and the sound of someone walking as they picked up the phone.

"Hello, Detective, you still there?"

"Yes, I'm here," Stearns said, quickly pressing the button to turn the speakerphone off and once again putting the receiver to his ears.

"Okay, I do have some records as far back as that, but I would need to black out the information we discussed."

"That's fine. Can you fax what you have to me?"

"It's kinda large. It's hard to keep help in the restaurant business. We see someone work here for a week or two and then just not show up after that. No phone calls, no nothing. This paperwork I'm talking about is like a hundred pages or so."

"Please, I hate to make you do this, and I know it's almost closing time, but this is urgent. Even if you have to send it in sections, I need the names."

"I'll do what I can, Detective. Where do I fax it to?" The owner sounded agitated.

Stearns quickly gave the fax number and thanked him. Setting the phone back down on its base, he breathed a sigh of relief. He was worried that the documents had been destroyed or lost with no way to recount who this guy might be. Stearns decided that he would touch base with Sarah again to see if she had made any progress while he waited for the faxed documents.

Walking back to the lab, he smiled thinking of Sarah. He had always had a small crush on her since school, but when it came to things like that, he had always been too shy to take the initiative. His relationships in the past, if you could even call them that, ended in dismal disappointments. He either lost interest after the first two or three dates or they simply found him to be too bland, too shy, or too committed to his work. However, regardless of the reasons, he had found himself slowing, creeping into middle-age status with no wife and no kids. Maris and Sarah were not close, and topics such as relationship status weren't really discussed. But, he knew she did not wear a wedding band on her left hand. However, he remained still too shy to ask her out and, more importantly, too afraid it would also end with other failure and be a source of discord within the department.

"Sarah?" Stearns called, as he peered around the corner of the hallway.

Stearns did not hear a reply and called out again. Still hearing no reply he walked a little further down the hallway peering quickly into the opened doors hoping to see Sarah sitting or standing behind one of them.

"Looking for me?" Sarah asked, giggling as she walked a distance behind, obviously coming from the opposite direction.

"As a matter of fact, I was," Stearns said, trying to sound serious.

"I figured." Sarah was holding a stack of papers.

"Well, good, no surprise then. I just wanted to see if you had made any headway as far as identifying anyone in relationship to the female hair you analyzed?"

"As a matter of fact, I am piecing together a few things, which is why I was headed to speak with you once I made a couple more phone calls. The name of the deceased is Connie Brown, a resident of Georgia, and I've located about four relatives; however, these records I am holding right now indicate she has a son. His name is Roy Brown, and he seems to have been the only one who was residing with her at or around the time of her death. When I had another officer call the local PD over there, they indicated to me that it appeared Ms. Connie had died of an overdose and no one, including her son, had been suspected of any foul play."

"So, where is the son now?" Stearns asked. "I'd like to question him."

"That's the thing. I'm having trouble locating him right now. The relatives we spoke to say he skipped town right after he sold his mom's house and collected the proceeds. He has not made any contact with them since. But I'm not sure if that's because it was such a tragedy or not. Sounds like a pretty dysfunctional family if you ask me. Maybe he couldn't deal with it any longer and just left town."

"Maybe," Stearns said, thinking to himself. "Maybe he did and landed in our town."

Realizing Sarah was still staring at him for a response, he smiled sheepishly and then cleared his throat. "I agree, that would be awful for a kid. How old did you say he was?"

"Oh, I didn't. Maybe early twenties I'm thinking."

"Any crimes committed?"

"A few petty charges," Sarah said, "but nothing too major. I'm not really surprised by that considering his upbringing."

"I'm not either," Stearns said in agreement, "but we all have choices."

Sarah nodded. "I'll ask the guys to call the DMV in the morning to see if perhaps another state license and tags were requested by this . . . Roy Brown. I'll let you know more when I do."

"Great. I'm waiting on some paperwork right now myself. You know," Stearns said as he paused for a moment, "you would've made a great detective."

Sarah blushed ever so slightly. "Don't flatter me, Stearns," her finger poking into his side playfully.

"I'm not," he said, stuttering, "I meant every word." He could feel his face beginning to redden so he turned his head slightly away to not appear so obvious.

"Well, thanks but I think I'll leave that up to you," she said sincerely and waved him a pleasant good-bye. Feeling like he was being dismissed, he shrugged his shoulders and walked to the break room. He had been so busy he hadn't even noticed the grumbling of his stomach getting louder. Until the Williams' boy was found, sleep and a good meal just weren't an option. Besides, he was anxious to see if his hunch was right about the restaurant. The fluorescent lights above flickered as he made his way to the two large vending machines in the far right corner. Although there was a large coffee pot sitting atop the adjacent counter, he was more in the mood for a soft drink and a chocolaty, gooey candy bar. Coffee would come later when the necessity to keep his eyes open was without question. Reaching deeply in his pockets he counted the loose change in his hand and made his selections. Grabbing both his treat and cold drink, he walked out of the break room and toward his office again. Fumbling to balance the drink and turn the knob, he finally managed to get his door open without the can falling from his hands. As he set it down on his desk, a red flashing light caught his attention. He was receiving a fax. *Hopefully, this is what I have been waiting for from the restaurant.*

Stearns sat down as he ate his candy bar and glanced over the stack of phone calls to return. It was going to be hectic, but everything else beside the disappearance was going to have to remain on hold for the time being. He glanced through the messages on his desk to see

103

if any of them was relevant to the disappearance. Noticing that Chief Roberts had left a couple of messages, he picked up the phone and dialed the Green Valley Police Department.

"Oh, he's not here, Detective Stearns. He left about an hour ago. But you can reach him on his mobile phone. The number is . . ." the dispatcher said, trying to be helpful.

"Thanks, I'll do that." Stearns quickly hung up in order to dial the chief's cell phone before it got any later.

The phone rang twice and then the familiar sound of Chief Roberts' deep voice bellowed into the receiver. "Yes, Chief Roberts here."

"Chief, it's Stearns."

"Stearns," Chief Roberts said, coughing a few times as he tried to clear his throat before resuming. "I tried calling you earlier but couldn't get through. Guess I'm not important enough to have your mobile number."

"I usually tell the officers up front not to give it out to just anyone. I should have let them know to give it to you when you called, especially if I'm not around the office. Sorry about that. What did you need?"

"Well, I was just trying to see how you were coming along with the investigation. Me and my guys are gonna be at the search location at about 7:00 a.m., weather permitting."

"I sure appreciate that, and as far as the investigation, I have a dead lady's hair and a fax that might have some bearing on the case."

"You what?" Chief Roberts said incredulously.

Stearns explained the analysis of the clothing, the hair strands, and the conversation with the owner of the restaurant. He could tell with the long exhale that Chief Roberts wasn't too convinced that anything he was doing would yield any tangible results.

"Chief, you can't tell me that you'd be doing anything differently."

"I don't need to add to YOUR investigation. It's your county, your case. My gut just says he is somewhere in those woods. If he ain't there, he's not anywhere around here. And if that's the case, then we need to call some people better equipped and with much more experience with these kinda situations than us."

"Agreed, although I think I'm on to something over here with the hair."

"A dead lady's hair? I don't get how you think that's some great thing."

"There is still a possibility it may lead us to the kidnapper."

"Are we still talking about the newest kidnapping or the one that was years ago?"

"Maybe both."

"Both? Stearns, I hate to tell you this but you and I both know that this kid is dead too. It's been days and there's been very little coming forward that's been helpful. I know. But remember, I was the one who had to bag the first kid. So, while I understand you wanna rule anything out, we just need to meet up in the morning and get this over with."

"Okay, Chief. I'll see ya in the morning." Stearns knew it was probably best to just hang up. Nothing was going to change Chief Roberts' mind. He was too calloused and too stubborn to think anything else. Besides, the red light of the fax machine had stopped flashing and Stearns was curious to see if the fax had come through. He went to the machine and looked at the stack of documents that sat in the tray. He couldn't tell if this was everything he had requested, but the large stack of paper was a sure indicator that he had enough to get started. Grabbing a handful of paper, he walked back to his desk and plopped it down in front of him like so many other documents before. Almost perfunctory, he sat down tiredly in his chair and began to fumble his way through. Sarah had told him that the hair belonged to a middle-aged woman named Connie Brown. Now, he needed to find something that might link this lady and someone she knew that was in direct contact with Ms. McKenzie's little boy. Problem was there was no real link to that murder and this recent disappearance. But something on the inside pulled at him viscerally, not wanting to let go of the idea that the two were intrinsically intertwined together, even if no one really believed him. Every other lead had left him empty handed and without any real direction to turn. The search was going to continue as planned, all authorities had been notified as was the usual protocol, and every possible witness was being questioned. *Why can't everyone just allow me to be satisfied that there is nothing more to be done?* he thought, trying to argue his point to an absent audience.

The papers had been blacked out in certain areas, but this came as no surprise. He knew some of the information was confidential and irrelevant to his case. Name after name appeared through the stack of payroll information. Assuming there was some sense of order, perhaps alphabetically, Stearns thumbed his way through the A's and into the B's, hoping that someone with the same last name would be here. Unfortunately, they were all scattered about—A's with B's, E's with Z's—and not in chronological order either. Stearns grimaced, realizing that he should've opted for the coffee as he began to feel further and further drained from the day's events. He began to tediously read each and every page. Some were easy enough to put into the pile of discard, anyone appearing years after really didn't appeal to him. What he was looking for was a male, late teens-early twenties who was working the night Tanner McKenzie disappeared. Moments later, he found what he was desperately looking for. He had almost scanned the entire stack and was about to give up and head home, but there it was as plain as day sitting near the bottom of the stack of documents. Stearns lifted up the sheet of paper and read it aloud, "Roy Brown." Stearns was elated at the discovery and then instantly saddened as he realized the prospects of locating Mr. Brown after all these years. Grabbing the sheet of paper, he headed for the department dispatcher.

"I'm gonna need for you to put out an announcement to all the officers that they need to be on the lookout for an individual by the name of Roy Brown. He may not be anywhere near here, but if he is, he's to be considered armed and dangerous."

"Is he the one who took that Williams kid?" the dispatcher responded eagerly.

"I don't know yet. I need to link him to Taylor during that time, which I'm not sure I can do. But I can see if he's ever been in this town. If Sarah hasn't left in the forensics department, please buzz her for me and get her to make some more phone calls tonight if possible. Tell her to call in some favors. I need anything and everything on that guy."

"Yes, sir.

"Just yes will suffice."

"Sorry Stearns. Will do."

Stearns grabbed the paper and raced back to his office. Since he has already called Chief Roberts, he dialed the number for Mr. and Mrs. Williams.

Luke answered. "Yes?"

"Mr. Williams, this is Detective Stearns calling you again."

Luke listened as he motioned for Linda to come closer so that she could also hear the conversation. "Yes, we're here," Luke said, indicating that both he and Linda were listening.

"Good," Stearns said, "I recognize it's late but I'm pretty sure you aren't concerned with all that so let me begin by explaining to you what has transpired since you both were in my office."

"Is it something bad, Detective?" Linda interjected before Stearns had finished.

"Actually, I wouldn't say that."

"Then, you found him?" Linda said, her voice choking.

"No, the search is still going forward and it's my understanding that you'll be joining me between 6:30 and 7:00 a.m. tomorrow morning. Am I correct?"

"Yes, we will be there," Luke said, trying to calm Linda. "But I thought you had something new to tell us? If it's not about Aidan being found, then what is it?"

Detective Stearns began going over all the events of the day including the visit with Ms. McKenzie and the recent discovery of the hairs.

"I don't understand," Luke said. "Are you now saying that this guy, Roy Brown, might have taken Aidan?"

"Perhaps. I know it's a stretch but I have everyone looking to see if this guy has been anywhere near Taylor."

"Didn't you say that this other boy was brutally murdered?" Linda started crying uncontrollably as Luke continued to question Detective Stearns.

"Yes, I did, but I still feel like—"

"Like there is still hope, right?"

"Exactly," Stearns said. "I can't explain it but I believe that right now, your boy is still alive."

"I feel the same thing, Detective," Linda said, interjecting herself into the conversation.

Luke grabbed Linda and put his arms around her as Detective Stearns continued to elaborate, knowing that she needed some reassurance in her mind so as not to collapse in sheer desperation. Linda welcomed his compassion as she wrapped her arms back around him in reciprocation, her body pressing hard against his.

"Mr. Williams?"

"Yes, Detective, we are still here." He knew the pause had left an uncomfortable silence. "My wife and I, as you know, are just absolutely drained emotionally and helpless physically. We just needed a moment."

"Take all the time you need. I just want you to know where we need to meet up in the morning and what is being done in the investigation." Stearns hated having to sound so apathetic, like it was all work, no emotion, devoid of attachments. But there was no other way. Anything short of a resolute mind-set was a cry fest and he knew it. The Williamses were barely functioning and would remain that way without real answers yet as to the whereabouts of their son. After explaining Chief Roberts' assistance and the local support of many of the residents of Taylor in the scheduled search, he could surmise a calmer tone as the conversation continued. He could still sense that the Williamses were appreciative of his advice and determined to find their son, even if the prospects looked bleak and their emotions were raw.

"Please just find our boy," Luke said, his voice faltering. Stearns could hear the desperate plea, and he closed his eyes trying to stop the flood of emotions that had begun to build up in him since the kidnapping. He was determined to exact justice and to hold accountable anyone who would do such a cruel thing. However, he could not let his duties become clouded by his emotions.

"You know that I can make no promises, Mr. Williams."

"I know," Luke said as he squeezed Linda tightly. "I just need you to know how much we need our son back."

"I already know, Mr. Williams. That's why I will be relentless in my pursuit to find him." Stearns hung up the phone and put his head down. These conversations weren't easy, and the pressure to find their son was becoming a very heavy weight on his shoulders. He needed to get some sleep even if his restless mind fought his body to rest. Leaving his desk as straightened as he could make it, he locked the office door behind him and headed out to the parking lot and toward his truck. Home was a relief and yet a dread, knowing that it only brought the end of another day without resolution. Moments later he arrived at his apartment and unlocked the door. After a long, hot shower, he headed to his bedroom where he collapsed thoroughly exhausted on his bed, not even taking the time to turn down the covers.

10

A loud beeping sound continued to echo on the nightstand by Stearns' bed. Tapping it sleepily, he rubbed his eyes and looked around his room. Light from the only window beamed its warm rays into the bedroom and into his eyes. He quickly stood up and grabbed a pair of jeans and a shirt from the closet and got dressed.

He had his teeth brushed and keys in hand when his home phone rang loudly, causing him to turn around abruptly. The bagel slipped from his hands and fell to the floor as he grabbed the phone, still trying to juggle his keys and flashlight.

"Stearns here."

"Maris, it's Sarah."

"Sarah?" Stearns asked, surprised by the phone call.

"Yeah, you know that hunch you had about Mr. Brown?"

"Yes, why?"

"He has a residence here in Taylor, or at least he did six months ago according to DMV records. I was about to send some officers to speak with him at the last known residence but kinda figured you'd want to head out there yourself."

"Absolutely. I was about to head out to the woods for our latest search efforts, but just tell Chief Roberts that I will meet him there in about half an hour or so."

"I'm on it," Sarah said. "What about the Williamses?"

"You can convey the same thing. I spoke with them last night and got them up to speed with everything." Stearns said good-bye and hung up the phone. He left his house in a hurry, the sticky note with the address in his hand instead of the bagel.

Down the road, Stearns called the department. The dispatcher answered and Stearns asked for two officers to meet him at the residence of Roy Brown. Stearns could hear the dispatcher relaying the message. As he turned down the road toward the address that Sarah had provided, he noticed his fingers trembling; it wasn't so much of fear but of uncertainty. He knew Roy may or may not be there and without an actual search warrant, he would be limited if Roy decided to avoid them. He could sense the end was drawing near and hoped that his worst fears would not come true. He had told the Williamses that he believed their boy was alive, and to a small degree he did believe. But he, as anyone else might, wrestled with the knowledge that the longer Aidan was missing the less likely he would be located alive.

Stearns pulled up to the address and grimaced. He knew it was an area of town reserved for the less fortunate, or, perhaps in Roy's case, the less deserving. The house looked empty and eerie. He walked around the perimeter. It was a brick home, single story with white shutters on each side of the windows. Not a very large home or yard. Stearns took his time trying to glean what he could without causing any destruction. The house itself was at the end of the street with the nearest neighbors being at least half a block up the road. Stearns couldn't help but think Roy had picked this house for that reason alone—undetected and solitary. He could see clearly every vehicle and if it were to even drive down a mere part of the way, it would have been easily spotted. Stearns knew if Roy were inside the house, his presence there was already understood. A chill ran down his spine. Was it at all possible that little Aidan Williams was somewhere locked inside? He had to get a search warrant and fast. He cursed himself for not having called the judge first.

As he continued to stare at the covered windows, he heard the sounds of the patrol cars.

"Dang it, what's with the sirens?" Stearns said as a couple of the officers got out of one of the vehicles.

"Sorry, what gives?" one of the officers said apologetically.

"This was kinda a supposed to be a surprise," Stearns said a bit sarcastic. "If he didn't have an idea that we were coming, he does now."

Stearns watched as the officers put their heads down sheepishly. He felt a bit remorseful for his quick temper, but if any of these new officers were going to have long-term employment with the department, they were going to have to think before showing up with guns blazing. He was of the mind that to catch this guy it was going to have to require stealth, manpower, and strategy. If in fact, as he suspected, Roy was the culprit responsible for both Tanner McKenzie and Aidan Williams, he wouldn't give up easily. There was not going to be the "Okay, you got me" speech. This was probably ending ugly. Stearns was almost sure of it.

He motioned with his hand for the officers to follow him. A ring of his cell phone shattered the silence. He glanced at it and despite the interruption his anger subsided as he saw that it was Sarah calling him again.

"Maris," Sarah said. "We got the results of the other hair sample back. I don't know how you knew, but it is a positive match for a Mr. Roy Brown. I had them run it twice and, same results. So please be careful."

"I will," Stearns said. "I always am."

"Yeah, yeah, yeah," Sarah said, trying to sound unconcerned. "Did the guys get over there? One of the officers told me you called for backup earlier."

"Yes, they are here. Although I highly doubt that our presence is a surprise."

"Have you called Judge Turner yet?"

"No, I honestly ran out the door after you called and raced over here. I was being too eager instead of being smart. Wonder if I'd be able to make a phone call in order to get what I need to look around this place properly."

"I dunno," Sarah said, trying to sound sympathetic. "Best thing to do is call him and see. Pretty sure when you tell the judge everything you have learned, he'll agree this guy sounds like the one you are looking for and grant you the search warrant."

Stearns mumbled something unintelligible as Sarah waited patiently for his response. Realizing that he was too preoccupied, she said quickly, "Well okay. Guess I'll go now."

"Oh, sure," Stearns said, absentmindedly still stepping through the tall grass in the back of the house. He knew he still held the phone in his hand, but he wanted to keep moving along with the other officers around the perimeter. Trying to do both just wasn't working so he finally said good-bye to Sarah in order to focus on the mission at hand. It had already been a few minutes, and he knew he still needed to get over to the search party, who no doubt was waiting on his direction and leadership. Chief Roberts was good but when it came to skills, he kinda missed the mark. He was used to barking orders, of course, but this many people from the town and surrounding areas was an undertaking all by itself. He needed an organized plan for searching that particular area, not wanting any of the searchers to get lost and lose their way, or worse, that they might come face-to-face with the kidnapper, putting them in a perilous and unnecessary situation. The way he had it all figured out was simple. He would divide the search parties into groups of seven with each having an officer assigned to them. Then each searcher would be required, after giving ID, to carry a flashlight, whistle, and pepper spray. Not knowing what to expect, put an added amount of pressure on him, but with this many volunteers organization was crucial. He wasn't exactly a fan of just letting average people try to pin down a child abductor, but having the extra manpower and assistance was also a blessing considering they were a small police department and they had a lot of area to cover.

"Stearns?" one of the officers said loudly, forcing him to snap out of his thinking and back to reality.

"Yes," Stearns said, motioning for him to lower his voice.

"What do you make of this?"

Stearns walked toward the officers and stared at the opening in the window. Leaning closer, he stood on his tiptoes and stuck his face up to the pane. With the help of the sunlight, he was able to fix his eyes on a few objects that he instantly recognized: a sofa, couple of chairs, and beer bottles littered all over the floor. All in all, though he couldn't make out much, the place looked dingy and deserted. Stearns still wanted to search it though, and a call to Judge Turner was the next step.

Judge Turner's law clerk picked up the line after a few rings and replied candidly that Judge Turner was in court and could not be bothered.

Stearns wasn't about to be refused. "I really need to speak to him, Dottie, it can't wait."

Dottie had been with Judge Turner for nearly fifteen years. She had heard that same request over the years by everyone from attorneys to those who could not afford one. Anything to get the judge's attention. "I told you he is in COURT," Dottie said, this time more forcefully.

"Dottie, this is Detective Stearns and it's about the disappearance of Aidan Williams. I NEED to speak with him NOW." Stearns tried to sound diplomatic, but it was a feeble attempt.

Dottie was taken aback by his gruffness but was familiar with the matter since she had been following it closely on the local news stations.

"I'm sorry, Detective. I will try to get his attention. It may be a moment, so you are going to have to hold."

"That's fine," Stearns said matter-of-factly.

Walking toward the back of the house again, he held the phone to his ear, pensively waiting. He couldn't hear anything except the music on the other end, but he could just about imagine Judge Turner being interrupted and calling for a recess angrily. Finally, he heard the deep gravelly voice of Judge Turner.

"Detective," Judge Turner said slowly, his voice resting for a second on each syllable.

"Yes, Judge. Sorry for distur—" Stearns said as he was interrupted by the judge.

"I already know from Dottie that this conversation has something to do with the disappearance. So what is it that couldn't wait . . . let me guess . . . a search warrant?"

"Yes, that is precisely what I need. I have finally gathered enough evidence to formally bring in a suspect. We are at his residence now and need your authority to search the premises inside and out."

"I normally would have you come in and discuss this with me in chambers, but seeing as how you are already there, I'm going to make an exception this time and issue you the order."

"Thank you, Judge. I'll have one of the officers swing by to pick it up in a few minutes."

"That's fine," Judge Turner said, clearing his throat. "I'll leave it with Dottie."

Stearns glanced at his watch. He was already supposed to be at the park with Chief Roberts to address everyone prior to the search. A quick phone call to Chief Roberts' phone only went to voice mail, and so he left a message figuring the chief would see the missed call soon enough and give him a call back. He had already informed one of the officers to retrieve the search warrant from the courthouse located downtown, so it was only a matter of time before they could officially bust down the door. Half an hour later the patrol car pulled up, and the officer smiled as he handed Stearns the paperwork signed by the judge.

"Okay," Stearns said, his eyes staring right at the front door. "Let's go." Detective Stearns pulled the 9 mm from his holster and led the officers to the front door where he banged on it loudly. After repeating this a few more times, he yelled out loudly in the air that he had a warrant and was about to forcibly enter the residence if there was no reply.

Waiting a few more agonizing minutes to give ample time for a response, he signaled for one of the officers to kick in the front door while he continued to aim his pistol in the direction of their entrance. A few swift kicks to the dilapidated door produced the desired outcome. Both the officers rushed in as they had been taught in the academy, but Stearns wasn't too eager. He walked in with caution and slowly began to see and assess the state of the home. As suspected, it was a squatter's paradise.

Filthy just didn't do it justification. It was and had been the kind of home that had only been frequented in times of desperation.

JUST FIND ME

He could now see more closely the tattered couch and chairs he had previously detected through the window. There were long slash marks in them, and some of the coils were visible. Both the other officers had their weapons pulled out, the other hand covering their mouths due to the stifling smell of old, dried beer. Additional unwelcome smells came from an old, outdated refrigerator that sat alone in the kitchen next to a small microwave. The stove had been completely taken out, but Stearns wasn't too sure if that had been by choice or the home just hadn't been for rent with one included. The floors were littered with the trash of half-eaten sandwiches, empty chip bags, and discarded beer cans. Stearns felt like he was in a giant trash pile. How anyone could live like this was beyond him.

"Don't get sick, don't get sick," he said to himself, still trying to check out all of the rooms without getting distracted by all the piles of garbage. Room after room was filled with the same amount of squalor and disarray except a small bedroom on the far left of the house. Opening the door fully, Stearns and the other officers met in unison, having already finished looking through the house and coming up empty-handed for any new clues. Surprisingly, this particular bedroom was marginally clean. Though it only held a dingy mattress and an old chest of drawers, it still remained uncharacteristically cleaner than any of the other rooms. Not a single piece of trash littered the floor, and the mattress was devoid of any sheets.

Stearns moved about the room, once again analyzing the floors, walls, mattress, and sparse furniture. Although there was evidence that no one had been there for some time, the drawers still had a few clothing items in them. Stearns pulled one of them out after putting on a pair of gloves. A few of the items fell to the floor and Stearns bent down slowly to pick them up. As he looked up to avoid the open drawer, he noticed a newspaper clipping attached to the bottom of it. Standing up, he pulled the entire drawer out and flipped it over completely. There glued to the bottom were newspaper clippings of youth sports teams. Studying the articles closely, he instantly felt his stomach churning. Two of the pictures had Tanner McKenzie in them, just like the one he saw in the house of Ms. Anna, Tanner's mother. The others were unfamiliar to him but revealed the other face he had been dreading to see—Aidan Williams.

"This is it; we are gonna nail this guy," Stearns said as the officers stared at the grim discovery. "Get this evidence to the department as quickly as possible, along with the clothes. I've gotta get over there for the search as soon as possible."

Stearns had no doubt in his mind that Aidan was in those woods after the recent revelation. He was convinced of it. Now he had the evidence he needed to arrest Roy Brown for the murder of Tanner McKenzie and the abduction of Aidan Williams. He knew Chief Roberts wasn't going to believe that his gut had been right all along, *but he will now*, he thought. He had the proof. The only thing now was to find him and bring him in for questioning. Leaving the other officers to collect the rest of the evidence, he got into his truck and put his sirens on. He was determined to catch this monster before he harmed another child, no matter what.

"I will hunt you down," Stearns said in the air as if Roy was in his presence.

Minutes later he arrived at the entrance to the park by the large, wooded area that separated Taylor from Green Valley. He noticed that area looked empty except for a few officers sitting in their patrol cars and talking on their cell phones. Stearns parked his truck and ran up to one of them.

"Hey," Stearns said, leaning into the vehicle. The young officer looked stunned. "Where is Chief Roberts? The volunteers?" Stearns was a bit out of breath and agitated.

"Oh, well, we waited for a while, and he decided to go ahead and begin looking for that kid."

"He what?" Stearns was in disbelief and tried to hold back his emotions.

The officer gulped, confused at Stearns' behavior. "Chief said he was ready to get the show on the road, and I think everybody was in agreement. Why are you so upset? Isn't that what we are here for?"

Stearns let out a sigh. "Yes, that's what WE are all here for, but I have some new information and it is MY investigation."

"Okay, sorry about that, Detective. I really am. We were only following orders. Chief told me and some of the others to stay here though in case you showed up."

Stearns realized the young officer was being sincere, and he began to feel a little remorseful for his irate behavior. "Do you know which direction they went? Did he have them split up? What time do you think they started?"

The rookie didn't seem too confident in his reply, probably because he had been fiddling with his cell phone and not really paying too much attention. "I think they went that way," he said, pointing northwest with his finger. "And they were in three groups. I'm guessing they left the parking lot about thirty minutes ago. So they probably didn't get too far in those woods. They had a lot of people show up to help search."

He knew the officer was just trying to be helpful, so he politely thanked him and went back to his vehicle, but inside he was livid. Grabbing his handgun and an extra magazine, he shut the door and began running in the direction the officer had indicated to him. Once this case was over he would deal with Chief Roberts. *Good thing I'm agile and used to play in these woods as a kid*, he thought. It wouldn't take him long to catch up with at least one of the groups, if not all. The chief had no clue what he was dealing with. Even if he were to find them, he knew nothing of Roy. This guy was heartless, cold-blooded, and downright evil. He would prove too much for the aging chief, who was not only slowing in age but expanding due to his cushy office job and weakness for sugary sweets. He closed his eyes and imagined the chief panting as he climbed from one hill to another, sweating profusely, and taking frequent breaks. Since he was such a glory hound, he no doubt would be forcing his entire group to patiently wait for his lead.

Without any hindrance though, Stearns was able to get his own pace and jumped from hill to hill quickly like a young deer. He tried to move fast but wisely, not knowing who or what might be just around the corner. Finally, after another twenty minutes of hiking, he heard a familiar voice.

"Okay, everybody, let's take a small break here and get our bearings." Stearns laughed to himself as the vision in his mind of Chief Roberts became a reality.

11

"Look who finally decided to make it," Chief Roberts said condescendingly as Stearns announced his arrival. As suspected, the chief had propped his large body against a small elm and was wiping the sweat from his forehead with a oversized handkerchief.

"Guess you decided to start without me, huh?" Stearns said sarcastically.

"Thought you just weren't gonna show," Chief Roberts said, not skipping a beat.

"Now, you know better than that, Chief." The aggravation was visible in his tone. "This is MY investigation, remember?"

The chief looked at Stearns. "Because of me, this search is actually happening right now. When everyone was standing and waiting for you . . . you were nowhere to be found."

Stearns glanced around, noticing that some of the people began to stare at him, obviously overhearing the chief's comments. "I was actually at the house of the man who took Aidan Williams."

Those who were within earshot stopped speaking and became still as Stearns continued speaking. "We were able to identify a possible suspect and get a search warrant for his residence. Upon arrival, we concluded that more likely than not, he is the person responsible for the disappearance of Aidan Williams."

Luke and Linda Williams, who were also in the party with Chief Roberts, stopped dead in their tracks as they heard Detective Stearns' words. But Chief Roberts did not seem too impressed with Stearns' verbal report and continued to wipe his forehead.

"Stearns," Chief Roberts said, pushing himself up and back on his feet. "We all know this is probably going to end up badly, so we might as well get it over with. Suspect or not there is no way this kid is still living."

Linda Williams gasped when she heard the chief's apathetic response. Unwilling to think of something like that, his response was like a dagger piercing her to her very core.

"How dare you say that?" she said, pushing her husband away from her as he tried to stop her from confronting the chief's unsympathetic comments.

"Ma'am," Chief Roberts said slowly, "the chances of us finding either the person who took your son or your son alive are almost nil. Surely you understand that."

"I am unwilling to give up on my son," Linda said, her tears beginning to fall down her face. "The least you could do is pretend to care about finding my boy."

Stearns was just as infuriated by the chief's calloused behavior, but unlike Mrs. Williams, he had gotten used to it over the years. It was hard to tell if the chief really was as insensitive as he appeared or rather that he just refused to allow anyone to see his true emotions. Either way, Stearns knew that if he didn't intervene, the emotions were going to paralyze them from any productivity.

"Mrs. Williams," Stearns said compassionately, "I am speaking on behalf of all of us, when I say that we are out here because we *do* care and we are going to find Aidan. Despite the fact that this search might have gotten off on the wrong foot does not mean that it cannot continue on the right one . . . that is if we are willing to put aside any differences we may have and search for your son in one accord. I may not have been here this morning as originally planned, but that is because I believe I have found the person who committed not only this atrocious act but one prior to this. I need to make you all aware that this individual may be armed and, with or without a weapon, dangerous. I would not want anyone stepping away from the safety of the search team and being injured. Please stick together and keep your eyes open for anything and EVERYTHING."

Luke shook his head in disbelief "What do you mean?"

Stearns looked at him. "Well, I thought it was pretty self-explanatory."

"No, that's not what I meant," Luke said as he walked closer to Detective Stearns. "I meant you said the individual had committed this kidnapping and one prior to this. Now, am I hearing you clearly that this guy got loose or something and took our kid?"

"Not exactly."

"What do you mean not exactly?"

"I mean that this man has never been prosecuted and that the other case remains unsolved."

"So, this guy has just been on the loose to basically do the same thing to someone else's child?" Luke's words hung in the air as he tried to not let his anger get the best of him.

Stearns knew that Mr. Williams was struggling with his composure. He set his hand on his shoulder, trying to think of the right words to respond. "Mr. Williams, the answer is yes . . . as sad as it sounds . . . yes. Sometimes, scarce evidence, certain technologies undeveloped, or faulty judicial systems can significantly hinder the prosecution of certain crimes. However, this individual was never arrested and 'let loose.' There wasn't the technology at the time to analyze what we are now able to do. Everything was handled as it could be at the time." Stearns debated throwing the egotistical chief under the bus, but the only thing that would do was cause more tension and serve to deter them from the very thing they had set out to do. "I believe that we are all doing as much as we can and do not need to lose sight of finding your son."

Luke and Linda looked at one another, knowing that Stearns' words rang true and that griping about petty things was not the issue. More than anything they wanted to find their son alive and be connected with him. "Detective, you are right," Linda said softly, speaking for them both. "Let's get organized and do what we should've done before we started."

"What is that?" Stearns said as more of the volunteers began gathering around them.

"Pray," Linda said emphatically.

"Pray?" Chief Roberts said sarcastically.

"Yes." Linda appeared unmoved at his comments. "Or is that not okay with you?"

"Oh, I don't have a problem per se, just don't see that it is going to do a whole lotta good, that's all," the chief retorted.

"I'm really sorry you feel that way," she said. "But this is our boy and I would like to say one anyway."

"Very well," Chief Roberts said, rolling his eyes as if he had been severely inconvenienced. Stearns smiled to himself, instantly impressed with Mrs. Williams' courage and resilience. Everyone stood still as Luke and Linda Williams bowed their heads and began to pray aloud. Stearns could see some of the deputies shuffling about uncomfortably, but out of the corner of his eye, even the chief had bowed his head respectfully. Once the prayer was finished, Linda rubbed the tears out of her eyes and gathered up the water bottles she had set down. She could see the looks on some of the volunteers' faces, some sympathetic, others merely collecting their things in order to trek further into the woods. She had prayed for the other searchers as well, but deep down inside she hoped that she and Luke would be the first to find Aidan and put their arms around him. *What if he's not here?* she thought, her mind racing with different ideas. *Don't think that!* she mentally scolded herself. Stearns watched with disapproval as everyone gathered up their items and began walking, with Chief Roberts attempting to lead them.

"Wait, hold up," he said loudly. Everyone turned their heads back. "This is never going to work."

The chief turned his head toward Stearns, not even pretending to stifle a sarcastic yawn before replying. "What now, Stearns?"

"If we are to catch this guy, if in fact he is really out here, then we are gonna have to have a plan of attack." Chief Roberts rolled his eyes and turned toward some of the deputies who followed close behind him. Tapping his fingers over his gun holster he replied loudly and sardonically, "This here is our plan of attack."

"Well, I just don't think that's enough, Chief. I think we need to fan out like a long line as opposed to just walking in a group. Each person will be about five to ten feet away from each other, and this way we can cover more ground in a shorter period of time."

"Well, we would've covered more ground if you had been here on time."

Stearns was visibly upset. "Chief, I'm not gonna argue with you. This investigation is being handled by me."

"Oh, really, so you wanna be in charge of this operation?"

"Chief, while I appreciate your assistance, I already am in charge! Now, everybody gather round for just a few moments while I explain what we need you to do."

Stearns had never been one to feel intimidated, even if Chief Roberts was throwing his weight around, literally. As a child he had sometimes played in these woods and knew that terrain for some of the volunteers would be treacherous. If everyone followed his commands, they would all walk at the same pace as opposed to having to lag behind in order to avoid any stragglers who were not keeping up. Besides, with the chief having to relinquish his authority during this search, it was less likely that everyone would be taking a break every five minutes just so he could bicker and wipe his forehead.

After Stearns had finished briefing everyone, he could tell that everyone's mood had picked up. By being organized, everyone in the search party not only knew they had a role to play but the importance of it. The chain had to remain unbroken as to avoid anyone or anything being missed.

"Okay, everyone. I think we've got it now. Let's spread out in a uniformed line. Remember, if you are not at the same pace as the person on your right, you have a problem. Make sure he or she is visible to you. Keep your eyes open and your mind focused."

The Williamses and others nodded their heads in agreement and began moving as Stearns had suggested. Within a few minutes, everyone had fanned out and was walking in unison over leaves, sticks, and small hills. When some of the terrain grew higher or harder to cross, Stearns would motion for everyone to take it a little slower until everyone had resumed his or her normal speed. Within an hour, they had already cleared more ground than the chief had all morning. Stearns knew that this fact was probably chapping the chief due to his overly large and sensitive ego, but he didn't care. There would be plenty of time to smooth things out afterward. Smiling at the progress, he made sure to make eye contact here and there with the Williamses affirming, even if only with body language, that he intended to search every rock and every crevice until they found Aidan Williams.

The trek proved to be more arduous than expected. Some of the volunteers were not in the best shape physically, even if their hearts were in the right place. Stearns who kept himself physically fit eased through the trees without difficulty, but as he glanced behind, he saw others were beginning to show signs of slowing down. Another hour later, he raised his hand, signaling everyone to stop and take a break. Chief Roberts was carrying a small walkie-talkie, allowing him to communicate between intervals with the other search party. Stearns debated about asking for it so that he could communicate directly with the other deputies leading additional volunteers, but thought better of it, realizing the chief wanted to still feel in control of things. He put his head down knowing that one way or another the chief, being the glory hound he was, would no doubt try to take the credit if the outcome was good and deny any part in the search if it was not.

Although the reality of this infuriated him further, in the grander scheme of things, it was of little consequence. He was more impressed with the Williamses. He continued to watch Luke as Linda would struggle a bit while she searched the woods or when she would smile encouragingly at him as she took his hand. These simple gestures he found reassuring and yet troubling, as he had never been married and there were no real prospects on the horizon. In his mind, an image of Sarah flashed and he tried to dismiss it. She was perfect for him, but the idea of asking her out made his stomach feel queasy. He was too shy to approach her about stuff like that. *Best to just leave it alone*, he thought, grimacing.

"Are you scared?" the voice in his head taunted him. "Afraid she will say NO?"

Stearns tried to shake the thoughts as he kept searching, but every day he was aging and having less and less time to start a family and raise kids. He knew she wasn't intending to be single forever. She was beautiful, talented, funny, dedicated, honest . . . all the things he was searching for. And yet, he never could seem to find the courage to see if she wanted to go grab a cup of coffee.

"Hi, everyone. I think it's okay if we stop for a moment and take another breather."

"Finally," Chief Roberts said, now perspiring profusely. From the looks of the other volunteers, an echo of the chief's comments resonated through the crowd. A few yards up there were some larger rocks and a few stumps that Stearns knew would make great places to sit so, ushering everyone a little further, he made his way there to rest.

Taking his time, Stearns passed out additional water and introduced himself quickly to each of the searchers. Disappointed no one had found any evidence of Aidan, he again conveyed his appreciation for everyone's continuing efforts.

"How long are we supposed to keep searching?" one volunteer asked, obviously just as disappointed.

"At least until nightfall," Stearns said.

"But don't you think we would have found him by now?" another said as others nodded their heads.

"Not necessarily. Folks, we have covered a lot of ground here, but these woods are pretty large. Chances are, we won't ever be able to search through them entirely in just one day."

"What about clues though . . . I mean, we haven't even found any clothing, the bike, or any other traces that he was even here."

"Like I said, while I would have hoped to find something by now to indicate that he had in fact been taken to these woods, we cannot give up. We still have some hours of daylight ahead of us and now that we have reenergized, we can continue looking. I wouldn't want to just give up when there is still time to search and he may be close by."

The chief scoffed at Stearns' earnest plea but surprisingly it was given very little notice as the searchers began to once again pick up their items, stretch out their tired legs, and move into their assigned positions. Stearns smiled again to himself as he watched the chief force himself to walk again. *If you're only here to take the credit, you had better earn it*, he thought, staring at Chief Roberts. Luke and Linda Williams, on the other hand, wrestled with the thought that, despite their belief that God would bring their son home safely, perhaps God's will was not their desire.

Please, God, Linda said as she walked over another patch of pine needles and twigs, *I need my son. I'm asking You to bring him back. Don't take him yet. Please . . . I'll do anything You ask me to do, but please spare my child.* Although her thoughts were hers alone, Luke could tell she was having another bout of emotions as she took her hand out of his in order to rub her eyes.

"Linda, it will be all right . . . really."

"Luke, I'm praying, but I'm scared. I'm asking Him to spare Aidan. I'm . . ."

"I know, honey. But I need you to focus right now. You've prayed, I've prayed, now you just need to give it to Him."

"Yes hon, I know. I'm just having difficulty because it's my boy and I just want God to let us be a happy family again."

"Then that's what you need to think about and only that. Whatever happens, good or bad, we have to remember that He will equip us for the road ahead."

"That's just it, Luke. I'm not sure if I am ready for anything other than good. I mean, He knows I am praying."

"Of course He knows, Linda. He is with us right now. We just need to be realistic is all I'm saying. I want to be able to take Aidan fishing and camping and everything else, but I also know that only God is in control, not us, even when we think we are."

Linda stepped over a few rocks as Luke continued to offer his encouragement and insight. She was grateful to have been given such a good husband. She shuddered as she thought of all the thousands who have their children taken and how utterly hopeless they are because so many of them are not Christians. Just then, something shiny caught her eye. As she walked closer, the shiny object disappeared from her sight, so she stepped backward until she caught a glimpse of it again. Motioning for Luke to get it, she stood a few feet back as he pulled and tugged at the small group of rocks it was lodged in. Linda tried to stay still as Luke buried his finger down into the rocks. Smiling feebly, he stuck the small find high in the air, his behavior causing everyone in the lines to stop and take notice.

"What have you got?" Chief Roberts asked, trying to be the first to make his way toward the Williamses.

Stearns was amused as he watched how quickly the chief could move . . . when his curiosity got the better of him.

"It's a coin," Luke said, handing it to Linda.

"A coin? Like a quarter?" the chief asked, beginning to slow down his pace.

"No, something else." Luke clutched it and pulled it in to his chest.

"Let's have a look then," Stearns said, now walking toward the Williamses. All the other searchers had stopped as well, as everyone awaited the announcement of the find.

"If it's somebody's loose change, I hardly think that's worth us stopping," the chief said, appearing flustered.

"I know, Chief. But it's not." Luke opened his palm as Stearns and the chief came toward him, revealing a shiny, gold one-dollar coin.

"Are you telling me I walked all the way over here sweating my butt off for an Indian dollar? I mean, they are rare, but it really doesn't mean anything to this investigation."

Stearns watched as Mr. Williams closed his hand and clutched the golden coin tightly.

"What is it, Mr. Williams?" Stearns asked. He realized that Luke and Linda Williams did not share the same sentiment as the old and boisterous chief.

"We are on the right trail." His eyes stared intently back at Detective Stearns.

"Why do you say that, Mr. Williams?"

Luke looked down at the small coin he grasped so tightly. "Because I used to give these coins to Aidan. Every year for his birthday, we buy him a gift and give him a few of the dollar coins. They were from his grandpa, and I have passed them on to him each year. Kinda a tradition between us. I believe, for whatever reason, this coin is his and he may have dropped it to give us a clue."

"I hope you are right, Mr. Williams," Stearns said encouragingly. "Although I must admit these woods and those coins have both been around for years. Many hikers, kids, and hunters come through here, and in all likelihood it could be from a complete stranger."

"My mind tells me the very same thing, but my heart is telling me that my son left it here. I can't explain why I feel that, but I do."

Stearns smiled, patting him softly on his shoulder. "Then we continue and let this discovery bring newfound hope and encouragement to continue as long as we have daylight." The crowd of volunteers nodded in unison and returned to their places.

Luke hugged Linda as he put the coin deep into his pocket and began walking again, no longer appearing exhausted or frustrated but determined.

Stearns knew that there was an hour or two at most before the sun would set, and they would have to venture back in a hurry to avoid nightfall. He had used the walkie-talkie to confer with the other search party, but they also had not found anything or anyone. Stearns was already debating on calling it a night, though he knew the Williamses would not be too keen on that idea now that they had found something they believed was their son's.

"Hey," one of the deputies called out abruptly. "Looks like an old shed or something about four to five hundred feet away. Think we should check it out?"

12

Aidan ached from head to toe, at least the parts of him that had not gone numb from sitting for so long. He was dizzy, dehydrated, and anxious. He knew that soon his captor would grow tired of hiding out and weary of being hunted. It was as if he could feel his life slipping away. A day or two ago, he had more strength and a lot more hope.

During the walk through the woods, he had lagged a bit behind. Having tried to keep his senses about him, when he discovered a dollar coin in his pocket he quickly dropped it only to watch it sadly slip through some of the small rocks. His captor had quickly crossed the distance between them, sensing his odd behavior, and slapped him vehemently, causing Aidan to lose his balance on one of the jagged rocks. He had grabbed Aidan by his arm, angrily forcing him back up to his feet and making him continue to walk, this time in front of him. He had watched a few movies where the cops had located someone after discovering a trail of intentionally placed evidence. So he had hoped that by leaving a few items here and there, he might be found before it was too late. Hopefully, his captor would not discover his plan. Like a human vulture, he could feel his abductor's eyes boring into him for any signs of noncompliance.

Much to his disappointment, after he had dropped another small item out of his pocket, his captor had crept up behind him, breathing heavily on the back of his neck. Aidan had been so scared he'd almost fainted. He could still hear the echoes of their conversation.

"What do you think you're doing?" Roy had asked him as he fidgeted with his knife.

"Nothing, I'm just tired and need to rest."

Roy laughed. "I'm thinking you're more stupid than tired."

"Huh?" Aidan asked, feigning ignorance.

"I know what you're doing." Roy angrily grabbed the small gum wrapper and stuck it deep in his own pocket.

Aidan watched him cackle again as he opened up the knife and stuck it in the air dangerously close to Aidan's face. "You will NEVER outsmart me. If you run, I'll kill you now. If you do what I say, I'll let you live . . . for now . . . so, what's it gonna be?"

Aidan knew he was lying, but running and being instantly captured by a madman wasn't an option. "Time is your friend," Aidan kept repeating to himself.

"I will not run," Aidan said, sounding convincing.

"That's a smart boy. See, I knew you were a smart boy."

Aidan knew his kidnapper was only toying with him but hopefully his dad and mom would find him soon and bring him back home. The sight of his younger sisters, even though they could aggravate him at times, would be a welcome one. The ropes seemed like chains now as his strength escaped him, making them feel heavy and cumbersome. The floor had become so dirty and foul underneath him that he gagged repeatedly. If only he could reach one of the shards big enough to afford him the opportunity to quickly cut at the ropes and free himself.

Another night had passed and he felt too exhausted to try reaching the secret space inside the shed. He needed water and he needed it badly. Perhaps that should be his first priority. His captor had kept it close to him, not letting Aidan near it, but if he were to inch close enough while his kidnapper was out on one of his treks to check his "traps," just maybe he could wet his dry tongue and muster up some strength to get home. The idea sounded appealing and Aidan bit his lip, determined to reach his goal.

The small container of water was nearly empty. Aidan knew if he drank it all and didn't get free, there would be hell to pay.

"C'mon," he chided himself, fully aware of the undertaking. The small glass pieces were as sharp as ever, and the only way to move toward the water container was through them slowly.

"Ugh . . . ouch." Aidan used his legs like a caterpillar by setting them outward as much as possible in order to inch his way further with his heels. The glass was almost unbearable, and he fought the urge to yell out in agony . The idea of just rolling over and saying a final prayer almost felt as if it would be a reprieve from the excruciating pain that he felt. Nothing he could have ever imagined in his life could've prepared him for the fear, pain, and despair he was now feeling. Tears fell down as he tried to muster the will to keep trying to reach the container of water. It was the only way. The chances of him escaping were already a small possibility, but with no hydration, even if he did escape, the probability of successfully making his way out of the woods and somewhere to call for help were almost nil.

Little by little he forced himself closer. He knew it was taking way too long. *He'll catch me*, he thought, his heart pounding so loudly he felt like it would explode. The water container was now almost within reach. *How in the world am I supposed to get it?*

The water container, if you could call it that, was nothing more than some sort of plastic cylinder that his captor had chosen to fill with water. It didn't matter whether the water was cold or even that it was clean. He only cared that it was water. Aidan finally reached the small ledge where it sat precariously, and after brushing off the bits of glass that clung to each of his feet with his toes, he used his feet to quickly bang against the bottom of the boards in which the small ledge was nailed to. The idea proved to be a good one even if it was elementary in approach. The container began to inch its way closer and closer to the end of the ledge. Aidan was still very scared that his captor may return at any second, but he was too far now to turn back. Finally, after a few more pushes with all his might, Aidan felt the water container fall and hit him squarely on the knees. It stung for a moment but was instantly replaced by the sheer joy that his idea had gotten the water down and now within his reach. Now, the next step was to move close enough to it, use his mouth to secure it in an upright position, and then bite down with his teeth in order to grip it enough to force it upside down and into his mouth. The first issue was just getting the container where he needed it to be in order to drink from it. It was easier said than done. He turned himself toward the container and realized he may have better results by using his feet. Although they were becoming numb again, Aidan jerked his feet violently, forcing the blood to flow as he fought the paresthesia and used them to tilt the water container.

At first, it slipped and teetered back onto its side again, but Aidan was unwilling to give up. He continued to try again and again until it was finally upright. The container itself had a small push top that Aidan thought he could get off with his teeth. So, turning himself sideways, he tilted his head as near as he could to the water and stuck the top into his mouth. His small teeth gripped the sides and he pulled up, forcing the top to come off and bounce happily toward the wall. Aidan then grabbed the container rim again with his teeth and quickly tilted his head back in order to feel the water pass through his parched lips and down his throat. Though he hungrily gulped down some of the water, the majority of it splashed against his face and into his eyes, and he tried to squint while still balancing the container with his teeth. There was more water on him and the floor than in his mouth, but he kept gulping while trying to balance the flask. He finally let it slip and fall to the floor when he had realized it was empty.

"Think, think," he scolded himself, grateful that he had gotten this far. He knew how long it had taken him to reach the water, and now he would have to work feverishly to cut the ropes and hide in the place he had seen before. Inching back as he had before, he picked up his pace, disregarding the stabbing pain of the glass as adrenaline coursed through his veins knowing that any moment could be his last. One of the shards of glass was larger and longer than the others, and he grabbed it behind him in his hands, trying to rub it against the taut ropes. It was difficult. Having to saw at the ropes was extremely tricky and time consuming. Although he was trying to hurry, the idea of accidentally cutting himself with the jagged glass was also something that weighed heavily on his mind. He could feel some of the threads beginning to fray, and he continued to feverishly cut at the ropes. Aidan's hands were aching and his arms felt very weak. "Don't give up," he told himself, thinking of his family, his room with all his stuff, friends, and all the things that he wanted to go back to. Finally, he felt the ropes begin to give way and pulled his arms around. The aching pain of doing such a simple movment made him want to cry, having been bound for so long.

Grabbing the same shard, he began hacking and sawing away at the ropes around his legs. Now he could feel the panic. It was as if his heart was going to stop. Every second was crucial. He could sense his captor was close, though not sure why.

Is he just toying with me? he thought, feeling helpless. Aidan kept on, not caring at this point about anything other than survival. Suddenly, he heard the sound of footsteps in the distance. The realization that his greatest fear was about to happen almost paralyzed him as he felt his hands beginning to appear unresponsive to his mental commands. He closed his eyes again, asking God to help him. Finally, he felt the final strand give way and he tried to quickly stand, only to find his legs buckling beneath him. He fell to the floor with a thud, the glass stabbing him through his hand when he tried to break his fall. The blood began to flow from the deep gash as he forced himself to stand back up and keep quiet. He instinctively wrapped his shirt around the wounded hand while trying to balance himself and avoid falling yet again as he walked as quickly as he could to the secret hiding place. He was inwardly pleased that he had been correct about the small and inconspicuous loft, which had remained undetected due to the overgrowth of plant life. His captor would have to look very hard to find him there. Aidan knew he would need to use his remaining strength to climb up in it and cover himself thoroughly. The feat itself would not be easy. However, had he been any taller or heavier, the loft would not have been a feasible choice.

Pulling his bloody hand out of his shirt, he brushed away the ivy and grabbed the small slats that were nailed to the wall in order to climb up. Despite his hopes that he wouldn't leave a trail of blood everywhere, it was obvious that he was bleeding pretty badly and wouldn't last long without medical attention. More blood than he realized had smeared itself on the dirty slats, but there wasn't much else he could do except hide himself quickly and hope that someone would rescue him soon.

Finally, up to the loft, he curled himself up into a fetal position, carefully making sure he had wrapped his bloody hand tightly in his shirt and fixed the ivy and foliage all around him while he waited for his captor to return. The blood was beginning to seep through his shirt but there was little he could do about it. Now that he was completely camouflaged, any movement might alert his captor to his whereabouts. Aidan tried to steady his breathing. He felt as if his heart was about to burst and, despite his efforts to relax himself, he could still hear the loudness of his breath thundering in his ears.

Suddenly, the loud and frantic footsteps of his captor drowned out the heavy breathing as Aidan peered through a small space large enough to see a glimpse of his captor. Without seeing as much as he'd like, he could tell that nothing short of rage coursed through his captor as he began to sling items around and cursing loudly.

"You'd better come out, you little brat!" Roy said, angrily grabbing the pieces of rope that had once held Aidan.

Aidan shuddered, watching his captor check the shed and then run outside, still cursing and talking angrily to himself. He was beginning to feel queasy. The blood was now starting to drip through his shirt, so he tightened the shirt around his hand to try to stem the flow of blood.

Roy, on the other hand, was beside himself, realizing that this may be the end of freedom as he knew it. He cursed himself for having stayed away too long, but he heard voices in the woods and had gone to check it out. Now having returned, his "prize catch" had managed to escape. *He couldn't have gotten too far*, he thought. He had left him weak and malnourished, thinking there was no way he could've escaped. *How is it possible?* The other boy had barely been able to move afterward. Perhaps he had underestimated this particular child. Scrambling to keep his wits, he stormed through the small shed, pushing back debris and kicking at the empty glass bottles.

"I'm gonna find you, little twerp, and when I do I'm gonna wring your neck and leave you for your mother to find," Roy said, screaming like a banshee.

Aidan shivered and tried to close his eyes, hoping that perhaps his captor's screams would alert someone to their whereabouts. Roy continued to curse and throw things about wildly. His behavior was more like a rabid animal than a human being. It was as if he was possessed with an ethereal fury unlike anything Aidan had ever seen before.

Nothing seemed to quench his wrath. Roy couldn't believe that a young boy had managed to outsmart him. He glanced at the empty water container noticing that it was empty. "Clever boy," he said aloud, realizing that now he himself would have no other choice but to venture out in order to find a brook or stream and gather some more water, thus exposing himself to a greater chance at being discovered.

I'm gonna get that kid, one way or another. He had come too close to let his perfect crimes become a noose around his neck. The boy couldn't have gotten that far, and with all the little surprises he had left for anyone poking around, the chance of him being caught in one was a good probability. Roy licked his lips and, looking once again at where the boy last sat, left in search of Aidan.

He headed first to the closest traps around the shed. Some of the smaller trees had been perfect specimens for him to attach strings of broken glass to and then cover them with smaller branches and leaves. The idea of the small saplings inflicting pain to an unknown victim with an array of broken glass delighted him, but realizing none had been disturbed made him shake his head bitterly. *I knew that little snot was watching me.* He crouched down to check the rest of the traps a second time, but it was no use. Roy stood back up and began walking hurriedly to the rest, still keeping an eye out for anyone who might get in his way. Although it had been a while since he had been in these woods with the other boy, some areas looked familiar and with his thin frame, Roy was making good time heading to the other traps. He had already taken his knife out, wielding it in his hand with the hopes that he would stumble upon the helpless boy and effortlessly finish the job. He was disappointed that he was unable to do what he originally wanted, but now his freedom might be compromised and he couldn't afford letting this kid breathe any longer. Suddenly, Roy had found himself in a situation he did not like—out of control, not calling the shots—and it terrified and infuriated him. It was a position that reminded him of being young, watching his mother's erratic behavior and feeling helpless and hopeless. The other boy he had kidnapped had been so timid right before he had finished him off, pleading for his life and to see his mother. Roy recalled the moments before he had watched his last victim's dying eyes close for good.

"Please, Mister, please, please, please . . ."

"None of your pretty pleases work on me, kiddo," Roy had said laughing.

"I just want my mommy, please. I won't say anything to anyone. All I want is to go home, I promise."

"You promise?" Roy asked, sardonically playing along.

"Yes, I promise, not a word."

"Okay, I'll let you go . . . 'cause you promised."

"Really?" Tanner had asked him, feeling some hope though he had already been abused, beaten, and severely dehydrated.

Roy recalled smiling, pretending to put the pocket knife up as Tanner had quietly thanked him for letting him go. Using the element of surprise to catch his young victim unaware, he plunged the knife repeatedly deep inside of him. Delighted to see the look of terror once again in the innocent boy's eyes and then resolve, as if his helpless victim realized that fighting was futile. He mouthed something softly as he choked on his blood and then closed his sad eyes. Roy had stayed with him afterward until he was sure it was over. No more faint heartbeat, no more labored breathing. Once he had satisfied his insatiable appetite, he had left Tanner's lifeless body for the animals to pick apart while he spent hours covering his tracks and any evidence that he had been there. However, in the process of getting rid of anything that might identify him or link him to the murdered boy, he had discovered the old shed.

Committing it to memory, it had been the perfect choice for this last captive, or at least he had thought. Whether he wanted to admit it or not, he had underestimated this defiant boy and his unwillingness to die. *But,* Roy thought happily, *when I do find him I will make him pay for his insolence, and he will suffer far worse than the other.*

After checking all the traps and noting no signs of tampering, Roy decided to return back to the shed in the hopes that the boy may have gotten lost, tired, and doubled back. Normally, he would have welcomed the hunt, but something told him that this was no cat and mouse game. He had underestimated the kid's resilience and now could feel his heart beating faster and faster as he retraced his steps for any sign of the boy. Killing him would have to be quick. Disappointed that he would not be able to do everything he wanted before sending another child to a shallow ditch, he picked up his pace, sensing the urgency to find the boy and silence him forever.

Meanwhile, Aidan tried to move himself around as he began to feel light-headed and more nauseous. His injured hand had been bound as tightly as he could make it in his shirt. It throbbed with intense pain and continued to bleed, though slower, despite his best efforts to stop the bleeding altogether. He knew he needed to keep his muscles from stiffening, but there was very little room to move about, and he wasn't sure if his kidnapper was really looking for him or was merely playing some sick game. He knew that in his present state, he would not be able to make it without medical attention. All of his previous thoughts of getting the water, cutting the ropes, and then dashing away were now a thing of the past. Feeling weak and lethargic, he closed his eyes. "Please God, I need Your help again."

Before long, he heard the familiar footsteps. His captor was back. This time, though still aggravated, he appeared less frantic. Walking about, he took his time picking up each item that less than a couple of hours ago he had thrown around in a fiery rage. Aidan felt the cold and calculating evil that permeated in the shed as his captor studied the water container and then the severed ropes that lay scattered about. Aidan watched as his face contorted back and forth, making it difficult to tell what he might possibly be thinking. Aidan knew eventually, whether he liked it or not, he could not remain where he was and if he wasn't helped soon, he might not even have the strength to get down. Though he wanted to cry out in desperation, he knew that to get emotional now would do little to help. He had to try to stay focused and awake, but it was getting harder and harder. His eyes felt so heavy and his body stiff and unresponsive.

Roy, despite his rage, took his time as he went through the weathered shed looking for any evidence that might be helpful in finding the boy. Though he had made a thorough search around the area, he had come up with nothing and no clues other than blatantly obvious ones. No branches had been broken, no footsteps in the dirt, how could this kid have managed to simply vanish? It wasn't possible, and he prided himself on having the last laugh. In his frenzy, he knew he had overlooked something, but what? He had made a mess of scattering things about but there had to be . . . Roy pursed his lips together and rubbed his fingers over them trying to think if there was anything in particular he had neglected. Turning away from the entrance, he bent down where his helpless victim had sat. The area itself was still damp from the urine, and the shards of glass were small and scattered about from his own rampage earlier. Roy tilted his head back, grimacing because the smell was almost overpowering. He should have killed the kid the day he took him, just like the other. Avoid any complications, cut off any possibilities of escape.

He had gotten too confident after he had eased his way out of the police's scrutiny. "No leads," he had read in the papers through the years, laughing each time and smiling sardonically. Saving a copy of articles he had pasted in a secret place to pull out from time to time to admire such a stroke of genius. He was not about to let this little weasel of a kid outsmart him and have him sitting in an electric chair somewhere. Walking back through the place where Aidan had been bound, he gingerly studied the layout. Most of the wooden slats were worn with a filthy, greenish overgrowth except for one area that had ivy from the trees overhead, which had grown down into the cracks and crevices of the old and dilapidated structure.

Roy began to walk toward the ivy, noticing that it was quite thick in some areas, almost large enough for a small child to hide behind. Opening his pocket knife and walking precariously toward it, he stopped dead in his tracks. Voices . . . lots of them . . . maybe a hundred yards or so away, maybe closer. Turning abruptly away from the ivy, he ran outside and headed toward his lookout.

13

Detective Stearns and the Williamses continued their search along with Chief Roberts, a couple of deputies, and a handful of devoted volunteers. The rest had met up with the other search party and headed back toward the park before nightfall. It had not been safe to have so many out now that the sun was beginning to set and many had expressed fatigue, so Stearns had thought it best to convey to them his appreciation and send them on their way. He knew that, despite their valiant efforts, many needed rest and had families that required their attention and presence.

Those who wanted to persevere for another few hours, however, were welcome to do so. He had planned to go on as long as he possibly could safely.

"I really can't understand why we don't just call it a day," Chief Roberts said, looking at Detective Stearns. He watched the large group of volunteers, ushered by a handful of his deputies, slowly fade out of his sight.

"Chief, you are more than welcome to head back if you like," Detective Stearns said. He knew the chief wanted to go home, but he also knew that the chief's pride would not allow him to show his true desire to venture back toward his patrol car in front of the Williamses. Ever since the discovery of the coin, Luke and Linda seemed to have gained supernatural endurance for the search. They were not as tired, as many others were, instead fueled by the hope that they would find their son here in these woods. Stearns, despite his aching feet, was also more inspired than disappointed. But at some point, if they did not find anything more, they were going to have no choice but to return back. Supplies, such as bottled water, had already been exhausted and now only two small bottles remained, hardly enough to do anyone any good.

"Chief, you DON'T have to be out here. If you want, I can take Mr. and Mrs. Williams and the rest of the searchers a bit further, that is, if maybe you can spare me at least one of your deputies."

Chief Roberts knew that he should try to continue, but not even his pride could make a louder argument than the arthritis in his knees screaming at him that his day was done. Tired, he nodded to Stearns, motioning for one of his deputies to stay with the search party while the other would accompany him back. Despite his desire to know what the final outcome would be, his age and weight had finally caught up to him, and even his own oversized ego had to finally succumb to the aches and pains of old age and bad eating habits.

Stearns and the others watched as Chief Roberts and a lone deputy walked back through the brush. Stearns couldn't blame him. He knew the chief was older, and he seriously questioned his ability to have gone any further.

Inwardly, he was glad as he watched them both leave. He knew that the chief wasn't in the best health and that anymore might do more harm than good. Besides, now that the party had thinned out substantially, and those who remained might not necessarily be able to cover as much area, they would, however, be able to move about faster. Picking up the speed was a necessity if they were going to continue such a grueling trek.

"Detective," Linda called, trying to catch her breath as she neared him.

"Yes, Mrs. Williams?" Stearns asked, looking up as she and her husband walked toward him quickly.

"We know that everyone is exhausted, even these brave few who stayed with us," she said, using her hands to gesture to the remaining members of the search party. "As much as we don't want to give up, we also don't want to put these nice people in jeopardy by being out here after dark. Is there something we can do to speed things up? Did anybody bring flashlights?"

Stearns stiffened his shoulders trying to decide the safer course of action. He had mixed feelings after the Williamses were adamant that the coin they had discovered belonged to their son. If it was true, then they were definitely on the right track and needed to continue. On the other hand, even if it was, that didn't necessarily mean that the little boy or his captor was still here. Only he and the deputy had thought to bring flashlights so no one else would be able to do much of anything.

"Mr. and Mrs. Williams, the most I feel comfortable with is searching no more than an hour. I can't in good conscience allow you or anyone else here to continue without proper safety equipment or proper lighting. Even if there was no issue of this very dangerous individual, the likelihood that someone would fall or slip and injure themselves due to the wooded terrain is too high and not worth taking a chance. I am so sorry, but I see no other option. We can come back out tomorrow and start again."

Luke and Linda agreed. Despite the sadness that lingered so heavily in their hearts, they knew that even though they would risk life and limb to keep searching for Aidan, they did not want anyone to get hurt. If anything, they were humbled and honored as they walked side by side with those they barely knew whose hearts were willing to help.

"Then let's make the best of it," Luke said, looking back at the remaining searchers with gratitude. After Stearns led them a little further without any additional clues, he glanced at his watch and shook his head. Calling everyone to gather around, he let them rest one more time before heading back.

Before long, everyone had rested a bit and was back on their tired feet. Stearns could hear his stomach making gurgling sounds, and he thought about how nice it would be to take a long, hot shower and eat a warm meal.

"Everything all right, Detective?" Luke asked, looking at him quizzically.

"Oh yeah," Stearns said sheepishly, "just fine. Let's keep walking in this direction. It should be faster since the day is about to officially end."

"Okay," Luke said. He waved his hands to signal the others to follow.

"So, do you think we will ever find our son, Detective?" Luke tried to continue the conversation. He realized that he and Stearns were out of earshot from the others.

"I hope so, Mr. Williams. Nothing would make me happier than to know that he was safe and back with you and your wife."

Luke smiled sadly, reassured by his words. "Even if he has been injured, at least alive . . . that's what I'm praying for."

"I know, Mr. Williams, and we will all continue to do everything we can."

"I know that, Detective . . . we know that." Luke looked over his shoulder where his wife and the others were walking. He was not paying attention. As Detective Stearns jumped over a small ravine, Luke tumbled downward, instantly using his hands to break his fall and hitting something heavy and hard.

"Ouch!" Luke said, yelping loudly in pain and embarrassment. Stearns had heard the commotion mere feet behind him and was first to jump into the muddy ravine in order to aid Mr. Williams.

"What just happened?" Stearns asked. He watched Luke brush off the leaves. The mud was all over his shirt and pants and trying to get it off simply smeared it further down.

"I dunno," Luke said, visibly shaken. "I must have just been too busy in my thoughts and lost my footing. But man, whatever is in that mire and muck down there cut me bad." Looking at his elbow, he saw that an ugly, visible cut ran across it. Blood began to pool and mix itself with the dark mud. Stearns quickly took his small first aid kit out and began to wipe both the blood and dirt away from the wound to better determine if he would need stitches.

Linda had also rushed toward them as did the others. By that time, Luke was more humiliated at the scene his carelessness had caused, but knew he should just deal with it and move on.

"Honey, are you okay?" Linda asked, worried and biting her lip.

"Yes," Luke said. He tried to act as if it were no big deal. Stearns had just finished cleaning off his entire forearm with one of the remaining bottles of water and contorted his face as he looked as the nasty gash on Mr. Williams' elbow and forearm.

"That's definitely going to need stitches, Mr. Williams," Stearns said. "What do you think you cut it on?"

"Like I said, I dunno but it got me pretty good."

Stearns walked over to the muddy ravine and took a long, thin stick to poke around in the place that Mr. Williams had slipped and fallen.

At first, the stick bobbed up and down with ease and the only resistance was mud and more mud. Then Stearns decided to poke more forcefully a few feet further and felt the stick spring back sharply. "Whoa, there's something definitely down there," he said, as he began to poke further around the heavy, embedded object. Each time he poked again and again the stick would bounce back in his hand. *Whatever is down there is rather big.*

"Any luck?" a few of the volunteers called out.

"Maybe," Stearns said. He tried to use the stick to get under whatever the object was. The mud was slippery and slimy and made it hard for him to maneuver the small stick around and underneath it. "Wish it hadn't rained out here and made a mess of things."

"Do you think a larger stick might help?" Luke asked, trying to be helpful.

"Not sure," Stearns said, looking up, "it's worth a shot."

"Okay, give me a minute. I thought I saw one earlier."

As Luke and the others walked around in search of some other stick to help aid Detective Stearns, he continued in vain to lift the heavy object.

After a few minutes, he heard Chief Roberts' deputy yell out that he had found one. Everyone had followed him back as he firmly handed the larger stick to Stearns.

"Hope this works," Stearns said, smiling thankfully at the young deputy.

"Hope so too, sir," he replied back.

Stearns took the smaller stick and set it aside, as he now made his way back toward the murky object and poked underneath it forcefully with a more substantial branch.

With a few heaves, he shoved the stick even further underneath and used his weight on the opposite end to push it upward. Before he realized it, the whole object had come completely up and out of the muddy hole, still dirty but with an unmistaken shape.

Both Linda and Luke gasped. There in the filthy mud was, without a doubt, Aidan's bike. Stearns forced the rest of the bike toward an area less muddy and set the stick down. There was no mistaking it now—Aidan Williams had definitely been here. Now all the pieces were beginning to fit into place. But where was the boy? Were they about to uncover a gruesome scene? He hoped not.

The searchers had now grouped together, with some making their way down to the ravine in order to help Detective Stearns pull the bike up for further inspection. Stearns knew that if there had been any DNA evidence on the bike after it was originally tossed down, it was long gone now. Getting it out of the woods was not necessarily his greatest challenge but more so the Williamses who were visibly distraught at seeing their child's broken bike embedded deeply in the mud and foliage. Forever discarded, or so his captor would have hoped.

Stearns felt around the bike, his fingers caked with mud as he tried to ascertain if there might be anything that was helpful. Luke and Linda Williams watched him closely, eagerly hoping that there may be an altered souvenir that may tell them more of his whereabouts, but it did not. The bike itself, despite its resting place, was still in good condition. Not much of the original frame work had been altered, only a little bent from Aidan's own father falling on it absentmindedly. Stearns brushed his pants off as best he could and shook some of the caked mud off his fingers. This find was valuable, but it had cost them some of the daylight they desperately needed to make it back safely.

Luke offered to help carry the bike back.

"I appreciate that, Mr. Williams, but it's not going anywhere. You are already injured as it is," Stearns replied back.

"This thing?" Luke asked, pointing to his elbow and forearm "It's no big deal."

Stearns smiled. He knew Mr. Williams wanted to help in any way he could, but the truth was that the bike at this point was of little importance in the grander scheme of things.

"I don't doubt your abilities, Mr. Williams. It's just that with daylight fleeting, we really got to get a move on, and the bike itself really will not help us find your son right now. I assure you that we can begin again tomorrow at first light with extra hands and more manpower and bring the bike back to the lab at that time.

Luke nodded in silent agreement though Linda continued to stare sadly. Stearns knew that it would be hard for her, but she would have to press on if they were to make up for the lost time since Mr. Williams' fall and the discovery of the bike.

"Will we be able to search again with you tomorrow?" Linda asked forlornly.

"Of course," Stearns said. "We will continue looking until we find him."

The other searchers including the deputy looked haggard, clearly looking forward to being back with their own families. If only they could find Aidan, all this would be over and then one way or another, the Williamses would have closure. He had additional misgivings about the boy's well-being after discovering the bike. Unlike the Williamses, he had seen the lifeless body of Tanner McKenzie, the viciousness of his murder evident in every picture. This man they were up against was no novice. He was a cold and calculating murderer with an insatiable desire to harm young boys and anyone else who would stand in his way. With every step and less protection, he felt more and more dread. Something inside of him sensed an unbridled danger, but as he peered deeper into the woods, nothing warranted such a resonating feeling.

Stearns motioned for the deputies to stand on the other side of the small search party. He knew that only he and the young deputy were armed. If for some reason they were ambushed, a plan of attack needed to be discussed. Luckily for him though the deputy was young; he clearly had a level head and a sharp eye. Stearns could tell that the deputy understood not only his position but the importance of it. "So nice to work with likeminded people," he said to himself. Stearns peered through the trees with their long, spindled branches. It was now dusk and the lack of light against the trees and other foliage began to play tricks with his mind as he and the others walked through shadows both tall and short. He continued to sense something sinister and scolded himself again for not having pushed the volunteers to move at a faster pace.

"Man, it's getting dark rather quickly," Luke said, trying to break the tension. Stearns nodded not really wanting the conversation to continue. He tried to remain focused as his visibility was compromised. He knew Mr. Williams was just doing his best to be polite. But this was no time for pleasantries. This was getting serious, and he needed everyone to be on guard and mindful of their surroundings.

Luke, sensing Stearns' agitation, decided it was best to just keep quiet until he heard otherwise. He had a habit of speaking when he was nervous, and right now the tension was almost overwhelming. After finding Aidan's bike, he kept thinking that every time he stepped, his next one would be over the lifeless body of his own son. It was almost now completely dark and though both Detective Stearns and the deputy had flashlights, it still had become very creepy and uneasy as they continued to walk through the woods. Most of the remaining volunteers were leery, huddling together, no longer searching eagerly.

"Maybe you can try getting through to the chief," Stearns said, looking at the young deputy.

"Good idea."

"I would like to know if he got everyone out safe and sound."

"Sure thing, Detective."

Deputy Fowler put the small walkie-talkie to his mouth and pushed a button on its side. "Chief . . . Chief . . . come in." Nothing but static echoed through it. The young deputy looked up at Detective Stearns.

"Try again," Stearns said.

"Chief, Chief . . . come in. Deputy Fowler here."

Still nothing but static resonated through the walkie-talkie. The young deputy shook his head as if confused. Double checking to make sure he was on the proper channel he tried again. This time, he slowly pressed the button and spoke loudly into the receiver. After no response, it was clear that he was visibly upset. Stearns knew that being out still so far in the woods might have something to do with it, but he wasn't so sure.

"Detective, I'm getting nothing. What do you want me to do?"

"I'm figuring being so far out here in the woods had something to do with that, but I'm not sure. Let's just keep our eyes open for anything that looks suspicious, and in the meantime we will just sit tight until either the chief gets back with us or we walk further and try again."

"You don't think there's any problem, do you?" Deputy Fowler asked, still appearing confounded.

"I always err on the side of caution," Stearns said, motioning for Deputy Fowler to hand him the walkie-talkie.

Although he was a bit hesitant, he handed it over to Stearns and stood still as the other volunteers caught up. Everyone circled around and watched Stearns continue to try to reach Chief Roberts and the others.

Finally, after a long pause, Stearns heard a faint voice coming through so he put the walkie-talkie close to his ear.

"Stearns, is that you?" Chief Roberts' voice was shaky.

Stearns pressed the button to speak. "Yes, Chief, it's me. What's going on?"

Chief Roberts coughed as he spoke. "The others already made it back. Me and Deputy Thompson decided we would venture further out, but we ran into a bit of a problem."

"What is that?" Stearns asked anxiously.

"I can't hardly go anymore. These old knees of mine have finally done me in."

"Where are you at exactly? Is Deputy Thompson still with you?"

"Well, not exactly."

"What do you mean? Y'all split up? Chief, you and I both know that wasn't a good idea."

"Stearns, I know you're not telling me something I already know, huh," Chief Roberts said sarcastically. "Look, my knees are giving out, my back is aching, and we saw that shed I think we had seen earlier when we were with all together, so Deputy Thompson left a little while ago to check it out."

"How long ago was that?"

"'Bout thirty or forty minutes ago. Kinda figured he'd be back by now, so I've been just resting about twenty or thirty yards from it."

Stearns felt a chill. "Chief, we are about half an hour away from the park. About how far is that from you?"

"I don't really know, Stearns. I would say if you were to head west from where you're at, you'd probably run into me or at least not far off."

"Okay, give me a minute," Stearns said. But in his heart he knew what he needed to do.

14

Every eye was on Detective Stearns. It was obvious that many were scared with the recent news, but Stearns always had a way of calming people down and looking at the issues objectively.

Turning to Deputy Fowler, who looked as nervous as everyone else, he pulled him aside and whispered quietly, "Okay, I'm going to need you to guide everyone back to their cars. It isn't too much farther, but I'd like to know I can count on you."

"Well, okay," the young deputy said, his eyebrows furrowed. "But, what are you gonna do? Go after the chief?"

"Yes, that's exactly what I'm thinking," Stearns said, looking Deputy Fowler squarely in the eye.

"But that's the chief. I want to help if I can."

"I understand," Stearns said, putting his hand on the deputy's shoulder. "But you already are by getting these people back to the park and into safety."

"Yes, sir. But you can't go out there by yourself. You need back up."

"I appreciate your concern, but I'll be just fine."

"Who's fine?" Luke asked, walking up to both Stearns and the deputy.

"I'll be," Stearns said calmly. "I'm sending you all back with Deputy Fowler here who will make sure that everyone gets back safe and sound while I head to find Chief Roberts and Deputy Thompson and bring them outta here."

"I can't let you do that," Luke said.

"*You* can't let me?" Stearns said, looking incredulously at Luke.

"That's right. If you go, I'm going with you."

"Mr. Williams, like I just told Deputy Fowler, I'd feel much better if you would both see to it that all the kind and helpful volunteers get back to their families."

"Detective, you don't have to go out there all by yourself. If Deputy Fowler takes everyone, then you and I can search for the chief. That way we can protect each other, no problem."

Stearns didn't know how much experience Luke had, but honestly he felt more secure with the option of Deputy Fowler. Mr. Williams, sensing Stearns' misgivings, spoke again. "Look, I'm not law enforcement or anything, but I can hold my own and I'd like to help. You need to have somebody watching *your* back. Besides, this is my son we are trying to find, and if we are on the right trail of the man who took him from us, then I'm going. Dangerous or not, that's my kid."

"I know that, Mr. Williams." Stearns' voice grew softer. "I just don't want any casualties."

"You won't have any!" Luke exclaimed, trying to assure the detective that everything would be okay.

Stearns really wasn't convinced, but even though he wasn't a father just yet he knew he would probably be doing the same thing in Mr. Williams' position.

"Okay," Stearns finally said somewhat reluctantly. "But you need to stay close to me and listen to everything I tell you. You have no real experience in anything like this, and I don't want to have you or me compromised in any way and wind up getting ourselves in a bind."

"I promise," Luke said, suddenly feeling more nervous than before.

"Good."

Stearns turned to Deputy Fowler, who was obviously just as anxious as he fidgeted his fingers. "All right, Deputy," Stearns whispered.

"Your orders are to go ahead while we stay here. Just keep the volunteers together and on an even pace, and you'll do just fine."

"Yes, sir," Deputy Fowler replied. He moved his legs around and stretched his arms out as if he were about to run a marathon.

Detective Stearns and Mr. Williams watched as he walked toward the crowd and began speaking with authority to everyone. Luke watched as his wife, Linda, shook her head back and forth in response to the deputy and waved her hands as if in distress. Luke knew she wasn't happy about their decision, but she needed to trust him. As he anticipated, she broke free from the small gathering of volunteers and ran to him, putting her hands over her face to cover the tears that were beginning to stream down.

"Honey, please don't cry."

"But, I can't lose you too," she said, her voice muffled behind her hands.

"You're not losing me. When all this is said and done, we will have Aidan back and everything is going to be okay," he said. He pulled her close, gazed into her eyes, and spoke firmly, "It's the ONLY way."

Linda tried to stare back at him, but it was difficult. She felt so torn—wanting to go with him, yet not wanting him to go. She kissed him fiercely and nodded her head in understanding. She knew if she did not begin to walk away with the crowd, she might lose all resolve and wind up running after him in resistance to his decision.

Luke watched Linda walk away with the others. Having been married for quite some time, he knew the agonizing emotions she was experiencing, but it was better this way and she simply needed to let him do what he felt led to do. Stearns, not wishing to get involved in the intimate exchange, watched as Deputy Fowler began leading everyone back to the trail they had begun hours ago. Turning to Luke, he motioned with his hand to follow as they veered in another direction—this time not only in search of Aidan but also for the other deputy and Chief Roberts.

The crickets and other creatures had begun their melodious hums and chirps as the branches and brush beneath them crackled a little louder than they hoped. Stearns had now pulled his gun out and surveyed the area for any movements or shadows that looked out of place. The lone flashlight cast a beam into the ominous darkness as they continued with neither one saying a word.

Earlier in the daylight, despite the possibility of the kidnapper's presence, there was a sense of safety that one might see and be able to avert any danger. Now that the sun had set and the clouds loomed above, the moon did very little to reassure them. It was almost so dark that had Detective Stearns not been shining the flashlight to guide them, Luke knew he'd have fallen again or worse, lost his way until daybreak if he didn't keep up. His elbow and arm still ached from the earlier fall, but he was not about to complain at such a superficial wound when his son might be injured or worse.

He felt a twinge of guilt as he stood behind Detective Stearns, having originally been skeptic of his abilities. Outwardly he appeared to be in agreement, but inwardly he felt angered when he had first met such a young detective who seemed to lack the expertise needed to track down his son's kidnapper.

Now, while walking through the woods, he thought otherwise. This man, whom he barely knew, was willing to risk life and limb to track down the person responsible and bring an end to the horrible nightmare. Instead of feeling that nothing was being done, he felt as if they were doing everything in their power to find Aidan, and a sense of gratitude swept over him as he continued to silently follow Detective Stearns.

Stearns could feel his arms beginning to tire, but he pressed on. The gun was bulky and he was not used to carrying it for so long. However, the last thing he wanted to do was be caught off guard and run the risk of being ambushed by someone as crazy as Roy Brown. The guy was a killer and sociopath. Stearns knew that if he was hiding deep in the woods, he was more than likely to behave like a caged animal and that meant all bets were off. He would lunge like a ravenous wolf if confronted.

Stearns looked back at Mr. Williams and whispered to him, "You all right back there?"

Luke nodded affirmatively, "Yes." His voice also soft and low.

"We've been walking now for about an hour, so we should be getting pretty close to locating the chief. It can't be too much longer," Stearns said, still whispering.

"Good," Luke replied. "I'm not in the shape I used to be, and this elbow of mine is starting to ache a little."

Stearns took the flashlight and shined it in the direction of Luke's arm. It was visibly swollen. "It looks worse than it did earlier, but it probably just needs to be cleaned more thoroughly, and I don't have much out here. Once we find the chief, we can head back in and if you need me to take you to the hospital, I can."

"I'm pretty sure I will be all right, just achy. Guess we need to be extra careful now. Do you think they ran into any more trouble?"

"I don't know," Stearns said. He eyed their surroundings and tried to keep his voice as low as possible. "My gut says yes, but I'm not sure why. We just need to find him and the deputy. They're both armed if I am not mistaken so if they did run into trouble, they aren't without protection. But you never know. This guy that took your kid is crafty and meticulous. He didn't get away with all this for so long without being smart, so we better not underestimate him. The chief isn't in the best of shape either and with all that huffing and puffing, he couldn't possibly catch anyone by surprise. In fact, I wasn't exactly too eager to have him come, but he has way more manpower than I do and I needed that more than anything because we can't catch this guy without it."

"And now? How do you plan on getting the chief out?" Luke asked.

"Your guess is as good as mine. I'm hoping he's rested enough to walk back with us."

"I hope so," Luke said. "Not sure I could help carry him with only one good arm."

"No worries, remember Deputy Thompson is still out there with him, and we shouldn't be too far from their location, or at least where the chief said he was."

Luke and Detective Stearns continued further until Stearns put his hand up to his lips, motioning for Luke to be silent. The gesture was immediately understood. Luke stood completely still.

Stearns strained his eyes scanning the woods until he pointed the gun toward an area that looked as if it had been tampered with deliberately. The leaves and twigs on the ground looked too precise as if someone had taken the time to set everything so perfectly, almost in a pattern.

Stearns signaled for Mr. Williams to not venture that way. "Just follow my footsteps," he whispered over his shoulder.

Luke wasn't really sure what Detective Stearns was getting at, but he knew he had to blindly follow. Walking specifically as Detective Stearns had instructed, they moved around the perimeter until Stearns finally stopped for a second to rest and catch his breath.

"What was that all about?" Luke inquired, trying to study Detective Stearns' face for any signs as to his odd behavior.

"I don't know if I'm being paranoid or what, but back there it seemed as if somebody spent a lot of time making the leaves and branches look so perfectly positioned. But for what . . . why go to such great detail unless . . ."

"Unless what?" Luke wondered why the detective had stopped mid-sentence.

"Unless . . . you're trying to cover something up." Stearns picked up a smooth rock about two inches wide and threw it directly into the area they had just avoided. The rock fell with a thud directly into the center. Suddenly, a small rope sprung abruptly from the middle of the pile with momentum from the tree's branch violently swinging back into place.

"A trap?" Luke replied, aghast at the recent discovery.

"Yep, I knew it. Told you this guy wasn't going down easy. Hopefully the chief isn't dangling somewhere from his toes."

Detective Stearns began walking toward the avoided trap with a smug smile on his face. It would take more than a few tree traps to make him leave. Taking his Bowie knife out of his back pocket, he cut the rope that dangled now in an empty noose and surveyed the area for any new movement.

Everything else appeared still but Stearns knew that Roy was close, real close, even if he couldn't see him.

"Stay near me," Stearns said, as Luke looked at the rope. "He's out here . . . might even be watching us now."

Luke shuddered. He wished he had his own firearm. Stearns continued to walk forward, though a bit slower than before. If there was one trap, there would probably be more, and with only one other man to help him, he'd best not fall victim to any of them.

He had heard nothing more from the chief and despite his determination to stay focused finding Aidan, the thought of others being hurt weighed heavily on his mind. Eyeing another suspicious area, he motioned for Luke to stay behind him as he threw another rock at the target. Once again, the sound of rushing branches cut through the air, this time swaying horizontally across as if to knock down an invisible foe.

"Well, that was close," Luke said, catching his breath.

"That's why I told you to stay close and follow my lead," Stearns said. He looked at the rudimentary trap. He had to admit Roy Brown was no amateur. Though his methods were cheaply made, his resourcefulness were worthy of remark.

"You keepin' count?" Stearns asked, trying to be a bit humorous despite the serious situation.

"I can," Luke said, "that is, if you think there's gonna be more."

"Oh, I'm betting on it," Stearns said with distaste. Even if they weren't caught by any, Roy had still managed to delay them in their endeavors and that was enough.

"I'm scared to step anywhere now," Luke replied. He tried to keep the conversation up despite the circumstances.

CARRIE SIMON

"No need to be," Stearns said, getting serious. "I am determined to catch this guy one way or another."

"Do you think you'll have to shoot him?"

"I hope not," Stearns replied. "But if it comes down to it, well . . . then I won't have a choice."

"I'll be honest . . . I've had to seriously struggle with my anger at the man who took my son. Earlier I had said to myself that I wish I was armed, but with the emotions I'm feeling right now . . . it's probably best I don't have a gun because I might do something I'll regret."

"I can't even begin to imagine how you are feeling. No doubt, I'd be feeling the same way, Mr. Williams. But you have to let the legal system do what it should. It is there to exact justice where and when it is needed."

"I know, Detective. It's just difficult sometimes when you wonder if the legal system is letting you down. I mean, I don't want you to take offense, but didn't it fail by not putting this creep behind bars from the very beginning?"

"I can see where one could make that argument," Stearns said after pondering for a moment, "but it's more complicated than that. We have requirements, protocol, et cetera."

"Sounds like a bit of a cop out."

"I sympathize with you," Stearns said compassionately. "However, it isn't. We always have to follow the rules and still protect human rights even when we deal with bad people. The criminal is not bound by that nor does he or she care. That's why it's more complicated as I said earlier. We can't just go up and grab anyone who looks like they might be a pedophile or kidnapper and put them in cuffs."

Stearns continued, "You and I both know it doesn't work that way. Although I didn't have anything to do with Chief Roberts' case, I'm sure he made attempts to put the responsible person behind bars. He just didn't have the technology, manpower, and other things that are now available to us years later." Stearns paused while looking around again.

He continued, "Besides, we are out here right now because some things, such as justice, may take time . . . but with reliable leads and devoted officers . . . even cases such as this can still be solved."

Luke knew in his heart Detective Stearns was right, but the anger and raw emotions were still there. He had continued to pray about it, knowing that though it was a natural human response, he needed to focus on his son's safety and not a pity-party.

His muscles still ached, but his determination to find Aidan one way or another was undeterred. "Okay then," Luke said with gusto. "Let's go get my son."

"We will . . . the chief should be somewhere around here too."

"Hopefully he sees us and we can get back on the mission."

"Exactly," Stearns said quickly, as he continued to keep his eyes open for any new traps.

***

Meanwhile, Chief Roberts was lying low, the battery of his flashlight almost gone, causing the light to dim and flicker. Deputy Thompson had left more than an hour ago and not returned, a worry for sure considering the recent discovery of the identity of Mr. Brown. But Deputy Thompson was a tall, 280-pound man who looked more like a professional football player than a deputy. *Pretty sure he can take care of himself,* the chief thought. He had to admit it was strange that he had not heard anything back from him, but he figured Stearns would be there soon, so perhaps Deputy Thompson was already with them.

It was starting to get chilly since the sun had set earlier, and Chief Roberts burrowed himself a little bit further against the mound that he had been quietly hiding behind. His rotund frame didn't exactly camouflage too well. He reasoned to himself if he lay still and stationary, he might just stand a chance of being overlooked by anyone who might be in a hurry, or so he thought.

Roy, who had been out looking for Aidan, had heard voices and immediately quickened his pace toward his lookout. He could hear whispers here and there with obvious heavy breathing that did little to mask its presence. Once at the lookout, he watched the law officers fumble and stumble through the woods like two children who had lost their way. He licked his lips like an animal studying his latest opponent, his knife out and ready.

Both appeared incompetent to him, one of which was obviously under duress due to exhaustion and morbid obesity. *This is gonna be easy pickins*, he thought, giggling quietly. He watched for another half an hour, completely focused on this new danger and no longer on the boy. As he watched, he saw the younger fellow pointing to something and then leaving toward the object of his curiosity without the other.

Roy wasn't too sure if he had spotted the boy or the shed, but the traps in that direction were in place and poised for an unsuspecting step. He would remain stationary and keep his eyes on the older gentleman. Perhaps he could finish him off before the other came back.

Initially, he thought there might be others but after waiting this long, it appeared like no one else was coming. When and if they did, he'd be long gone with no "loose ends."

Satisfied that this was the only way, he crept from his lookout like a cat slinking its way toward its prey. His anger and rage toward his young captive would have to be appeased . . . but later. The leaves were dry in that area so he would have to be extra careful where he stepped or the advantage would not be his. He had watched his rather unsightly target burrow his obese body against a large mound in an effort to hide, and he smiled with anticipation. It would take him no more than a few minutes to close the distance and then hunt the other one. It frustrated him that he now had three to kill, but no one was taking him to stand at trial for murder. He'd be "fried" for sure.

Keeping his breathing low and measured, he continued to creep his way toward the chief, who, never sensing the immediate danger, rubbed his knees in pain and frustration.

***

Stearns, hearing the faint rustling of leaves, pushed Luke with his hand and shined the flashlight toward the sound. "Stay back," he said, not sure what the light would reveal. He knew that Luke was unarmed.

The beam of light revealed a rather oversized mound with a strange figure leaning against it.

"Chief?" Stearns called out. He and Luke kept walking.

"Stearns, that you? Taking your sweet time, eh?"

Stearns tried to swallow the growing desire to snap back at the chief who clearly was in this predicament by his own choice and, as usual, not necessarily grateful.

"Yes it's me, Chief. Deputy Thompson isn't back yet?"

"Nope, he headed toward that old shed up there, and I haven't seen or heard from him since."

Stearns beamed his light in the direction of the chief's hand and then back to where they were standing. "Okay, just stay put and we will go check it out."

15

"What do you mean 'check it out'?" Chief Roberts said angrily. "Don't you see me . . . I'm about to fall apart right where I am, and you want to keep searching? As far as I'm concerned, it's time to go home."

"Well, it's not up to you. We are gonna locate Deputy Thompson and then decide how to proceed."

"W–h–a–t?" Chief Roberts asked in disbelief. "In case you haven't looked around lately, it's too dark to do much of anything. Besides, Thompson is a big ole boy and I'm sure he can take care of himself. Probably made it back to his patrol car and left me here on purpose."

"I doubt that very seriously, Chief. I've met Deputy Thompson a few times and although he might not be the brightest bulb . . . he's loyal." Stearns tried to contain the frustration bubbling up inside of him as Chief Roberts continued, as usual, to worry about nothing more than his own skin.

Even Luke sat aghast at the chief's comments. Sure, he had heard a few rumors about the chief's gruff demeanor, but never in a billion years did he think the chief might actually leave one of his deputies behind. Even if he thought he'd skedaddled, he had a duty to make sure everyone was accounted for.

"I know you think I'm just a no-good guy, but I'm tired, achy, and hungry, so I ain't wanting to go any further in these woods."

Stearns looked at Luke and then the chief. "Well, we all are . . . so you can either sit here and we will come back for you after we find Deputy Thompson, or you can muster some strength and come with us. Your call, Chief."

Chief Roberts bowed his head, none too happy with either option. He was getting too old to weather the elements, and the pain in his knees was now excruciating. Secretly, he admired Stearns' tenacity, but he wasn't about to let him know. He enjoyed being ornery far more than opening up to people. In fact, he'd become quite good at annoying people enough to be left alone.

"Well, fellows, guess you guys will just have to hightail it back and come get me once you are done poking around, 'cause this old bloodhound is too tired for another hunt. If you don't come back within an hour, then I'll head through those trees over there and back into town. Even if my knees give way and I gotta crawl outta here."

"Fair enough," Stearns said, somewhat amused at the chief's comments. Looking at his clock, he questioned Chief Roberts again about the specifics of the deputy's departure and quietly began walking in that direction with Luke trailing cautiously behind. The evidence of someone or something walking through that particular area was so apparent, as broken tree branches and marks in the soil appeared all around, leaving Stearns and Luke to ponder whether it had been Deputy Thompson or someone else. Stearns decided to bend down at one of the partial footprints and see if he could deduce anything from it. Luke, on the other hand, stayed standing, more afraid of what else was looming in the darkness. Stearns appeared unperturbed as he studied the print in the dark soil. "It's definitely a boot imprint and from the width and length, it clearly belongs to an adult male. Think we're on the right path. It appears that this individual wasn't worried about leaving tracks, so my guess is it belongs to Deputy Thompson. If he was simply meandering this way to check things out, it would explain the lack of stealth."

"Yeah, but we're almost to that shed or whatever it is up there, and we haven't seen hide nor hair of him. Do you think he got caught in one of those traps we just passed not that long ago?"

"It's possible but if he had been injured he'd probably yelp loud enough to be heard."

"Maybe, but not if he didn't want to give away his position and be under the mercy of the madman."

"Good point," Stearns said, still shining the light toward the shed. "Perhaps we will get more answers there."

Luke felt a cold chill, still trying to shake the feeling that they were missing something. He and Stearns weren't about to give up now that his son's safety may be merely a few decisions away, but something felt all wrong and he couldn't really identify the culprit.

***

Roy, in the meantime, was on a different hunt. He strained his eyes, watching the other two men leave the area. Angry that there were more, he still wanted to finish them all off, even if it took him all night to hunt them down. Now, no more than twenty feet away, he crept ever so slightly, using his toes to quietly push back the leaves and then extend his foot down on the soil below. It was a tedious process but cunning was something Roy had prided himself on. Extracting his knife forward in the air, he continued to inch his way closer and closer, his heart beating slow and steady like a seasoned hunter. He could hear the labored breathing of his target and realized that he was much larger now that he had almost closed the distance between them. *Gonna have to stab him a few times*, Roy thought, grimacing at the prospect that it would take more than one good clean slice. With less than two or three feet now between him and his oversized prize, Roy lunged viciously at the chief who was still hunkered down and trying to rest his achy body.

The knife instantly found its mark, and Roy proceeded to pull it out and thrust it in him again. But the chief, reeling from the surprise and pain, bellowed like an angry grizzly.

"Awwwh!" The chief's yells echoed through the woods.

***

Stearns, who was still bending down at the discovered footprints, instantly sprang to his feet.

"What the heck was that?" Luke asked, trying not to panic.

"It's gotta be the chief. I knew we shouldn't have left him there. C'mon and hurry . . . we may be too late."

Luke and Stearns began to run back frantically in the direction they came, the flashlight bobbing up and down as Stearns pulled the strap off his holster in order to get his firearm ready. Luke had difficulty trying to keep up with the detective's pace. He knew time was of the essence but the adrenaline coursing through him made him feel uneasy knowing he was not trained for any of this. His own heart felt as if it would stop at any minute because of the furious beating within him. He could only imagine the fear that must have gripped his son.

Stearns, on the other hand, despite his nervousness, ran with the speed of a gazelle. While he did technically have a "desk job," he tried to maintain an active schedule unlike some of his friends on the force. Despite their playful teasing of him, this was proof that maintaining a healthy and consistent lifestyle really did make a difference. He hoped Mr. Williams was doing his best to keep up. While he wanted to be assured of this, the idea of a murder taking place at that very moment fueled him to get there as fast as he could without worrying too much about anything else.

***

"Ahhhhh!" The blood-curdling scream rang out again as Roy continued to stab the knife deep into the chief's side. He could feel the blood spurting onto his hand and the hilt of the knife, but it didn't seem to bother him in the slightest. Chief Roberts struggled to turn himself toward the man trying to kill him, but his legs were already weak and his arms limp. He didn't know if he had been stabbed in those areas, but he knew he had to try to fight back. Willing the strength within, he pushed Roy back fiercely, the knife still in his attacker's hand. His vision was becoming blurry, and he struggled in a bloody daze to stand his ground.

"Why don't you just make it easy on yourself, old-timer," Roy sneered.

"You'd like that wouldn't you, you poor excuse for a human being," the chief growled in response.

"Well, you might be a big ole pig, but I say it's slaughtering time. So you can go down nicely or I can keep going until you beg me to finish you off. Your choice."

Chief Roberts coughed while trying to retort, the taste of blood in his mouth. "Then you don't know . . . who . . . you're . . . messing with!" His voice oddly sounded like someone else as he tried to spit out the pooling blood. He felt as if he were suffocating or drowning. He knew that if Stearns didn't find him soon, he was a goner. But he would try to hold out as long as he could, even if the truth was that he was fading fast and any moment could be his last. *Nobody is taking out the "Bear Paw" without a fight*, he thought.

Roy lunged at him again, and the chief tried to fight him off with all his might, miraculously finding the strength to block the knife after such vicious attacks. But this only seemed to anger Roy more, and again he thrust the knife forward, aiming for Chief Roberts' neck. Though dangerously close, he missed again, allowing the chief to put his arms up as best he could in defense.

***

Stearns and Luke could see movement in the distance, but it was difficult to identify who was winning. The shadows of two men fought ferociously until Stearns, who was now almost close enough to intervene, shined the flashlight directly in the direction of Roy and pulled the gun out, pointing it at him.

"Stop or I'll shoot!" Stearns shouted.

"You ain't gonna do that, 'cause if ya do then I'm not going to tell you what I did with the kid," Roy said, looking more like a rabid dog than a man.

Stearns debated about whether to put the gun down, but this was nothing more than a classic game of chicken to see who would blink first. Good for him that he knew the psyche of Roy, which gave him an advantage since Roy clearly did not know anything about him.

"No deal, Roy," Stearns said. The gun was still aimed.

"How do you know my name?" Roy replied in disbelief.

"Oh, I know a lot about you, so you might as well turn yourself in and avoid a bullet or two."

Roy licked his lips as he always did when he was thinking. Trying to sum this guy up was difficult, and inwardly he wasn't sure about doubting this man. Normally, he could tell when somebody was bluffing, but his gut told him this guy would probably shoot and it may benefit him if he conceded . . . at least for now.

"All right," Roy said after an orchestrated yawn. He then pointed the bloody knife in the chief's direction. "This guy is dead anyway." Stearns and Luke continued to stare with horror as Chief Roberts lay slumped over, his shirt covered in dark blood.

Stearns knew he didn't have much time and having the chief make it long enough for any paramedics was a wishful thought. Meanwhile, Roy seemed to be enjoying the reaction he had caused, and he playfully danced in a small circle, happy with his handiwork and seemingly oblivious to the gun still pointed at him.

Stearns' face formed into a disgusted scowl as he inched closer to Roy, ready to unload his firearm if necessary. His hands were a bit sweaty but remained steady. He signaled for Luke to run behind him and toward the chief.

"Back up," Stearns said forcefully. He made Roy move a bit further away from the chief who now appeared unconscious. Luke was now able to venture nearer to the dying chief and check his vitals. As he knelt down, he felt queasy looking at the amount of blood on the chief's body.

"Hang on, Chief," Luke said, almost in tears as he tried to offer some support. The chief did not respond, but Luke still gripped his swollen and severely bruised hand, continuing to speak calm, comforting words to him. He knew Stearns had the harder part of taking Roy into custody, but in all his years, he'd never watched someone die before, and it truly saddened him despite the immediate threat that had kept his heart racing. In his mind, he could only imagine what this psychopath had done to Aidan. The anger he had spoken of earlier began to return as he stayed kneeling by Chief Roberts' side.

"Well, what are you planning to do now?" Roy demanded, his hands still in the air.

"Drop the knife and lay down flat on the ground. NOW!" Stearns yelled unamused.

"Afraid I can't do that," Roy said with an evil glint in his eyes.

"Well, then you can go down the hard way," Stearns said angrily. "Doesn't really matter to me."

"Oh, I know better than that . . . you fellows got protocol to follow. Nobody's roughing me up and NOBODY is taking me in."

"Oh yes we are, and all you are doing is making it harder on yourself."

"I'm not buying it," Roy said laughing.

"Frankly, I'm not too concerned what you're 'buying.' This is the way it's going to be or you aren't gonna be given the choice again."

"Come and make me then," Roy said mockingly. Stearns walked closer to him. Giggling again to himself, a small fear still existed deep within Roy that somehow Aidan had managed to get out safely, thus no longer being a bargaining chip for his own life. But despite the spiraling plans he had for the boy, he believed that Aidan was still in the woods and just lost. With him being the only person who knew where he'd been kept, the police would be less likely to just shoot him with the understanding that he might be the only clue.

Stearns also knew that, to some degree, Roy was holding the cards, but he wasn't about to roll over and admit defeat. While he had a law officer dying and a missing child, he was banking that despite his big talk, not even Roy wanted to really look down the barrel of a gun.

He could tell that Roy was exhausted from the recent fight and was probably dehydrated from his stint in the woods. Though he was a bit winded himself, he was sure that he could take a man like Roy down. Keeping the gun pointed, he lunged forward as Roy veered back.

Luke, who had been watching the confrontation, rose bravely to aid Detective Stearns. The plan worked. Stearns was still with his firearm, and Luke courageously surrounded their would-be attacker.

Roy seemed caught off guard by the selfless gesture and turned to face Luke squarely. "You . . . you look familiar," Roy said, trying to delve into his memory for the answer to his recognition. "Ha, ha, ha, ha," he laughed loudly. "You're the kid's father, aren't ya?"

Luke bit into his lip, painfully trying to keep his composure. Stearns cleared his throat, indicating to Luke not to speak.

Roy, on the other hand, found this amusing and continued to berate them.

Suddenly, Luke had had enough of the tirades and lunged at Roy. The distraction was just enough for Detective Stearns to push Roy from behind, knocking him to the ground face forward, and quickly putting one of his knees squarely into his back, thus pinning him down as he wailed, kicked, and fought viciously.

"Get off of ME!" Roy screamed, spitting and cursing in defiance.

"Not likely," Stearns said. He steadied the end of the flashlight in his mouth while grabbing the handcuffs he seldom used from the back of his belt. Roy continued to flail his arms and legs about, but once

Stearns caught one of his arms, he put the handcuff on and forced it behind Roy's back.

"Ouch!" Roy complained. "You're hurting me!"

"Yeah right," Stearns replied, further disgusted by Roy's antics. Slipping the remaining handcuff on Roy's other wrist, a wave of relief crashed over him. But he knew this wasn't time to celebrate.

Luke ran back to Chief Roberts, who was unconscious. He quickly felt for a pulse and was surprised to find one, though faint. "Don't let go," Luke said, though the chief remained unresponsive. Roy was still wiggling, but not as much. Stearns, not too eager to have him on his feet, left Roy to squirm face down in the dirt and dry leaves while he walked over to the dying chief to see what could be done.

"Well?" Stearns asked, looking at Luke.

"I don't think he will make it. Do you see the amount of blood everywhere?" Luke exclaimed.

"I know, I'm just thinking if you were to call the paramedics now that we have him in custody, perhaps by venturing further that way over there to get better reception," Stearns pointed, "you could meet them and guide them back to the chief. It's a slim chance, but we owe it to him. He's tough and ornery, but he risked his life."

"What are you going to do after I go in search of medical attention?" Luke said, feeling confused.

"I'm going to deal with Mr. Brown." His eyes glanced over as Roy continued to fumble around in the dirt.

"But I want to go with you and find my son."

"I know you do, Mr. Williams, but that's unreasonable by any standards and you know that." Stearns voice rose.

Luke knew he needed to heed the advice. Pulling a small phone out of his pocket, he walked away dialing 9-1-1. The dispatcher answered immediately and though the reception was still poor, Luke was able to explain what had happened and where they were. "Please hurry!" he exclaimed as he hung up the phone. "Guess I'd better head the way you suggested and try to guide them back. Problem is . . . I don't have another flashlight."

Stearns looked around and walked toward the chief. A small flashlight was attached to his belt. Stearns pulled it out and handed it to Luke. Blood spatter was all over it and Luke grimaced.

"C'mon, give it here," Stearns said, grabbing it and wiping it off with the bottom of his shirt.

Luke took it back and turned it on to make sure it worked. The light was dim as if the battery was low, but it would be enough for the medics to see him. Stearns had guided him in a specific direction, but Luke was still as lost as a goose. It had been hard to walk away as Stearns sat by the dying chief and Roy began to curse and threaten even louder.

Now he knew how Linda had felt. Linda. He needed to call her and let her know what had happened. Holding the flashlight in one hand he dialed the number and pressed the phone to his ear in the other.

"Linda?" Luke said after the phone rang once.

"Luke? Where are you? What are you doing using the phone? Are you still in the woods? I thought Detective Stearns told us to turn all the cell phones off and not use them?"

"I know he did, but we can use them now."

"What do you mean?" Linda asked, her thoughts running rampant. "Please tell me you found Aidan."

Luke let out a long breath. "No . . . Linda, I wish I could. Believe me—"

"Then what happened?"

"We have the guy, who took Aidan, in handcuffs."

Linda suddenly became quiet. "Did you ask him where our son is?"

"No."

"Why?"

"I couldn't."

"What do you mean you couldn't?"

"I couldn't . . . It's complicated."

"Complicated? How is walking up to the creep and demanding that he tell us where Aidan is complicated? Luke, you're not making any sense."

"Honey, I can't go into all that right now. Please, I'm asking you again to just trust me. Are you still walking?"

"No, but we made it back to the clearing already. I'm about to call my mother and tell her to keep the girls over there tonight. I can't bear to tuck them in and tell them we didn't find Aidan." Linda's voice wavered as she spoke full of emotion.

"That's good. I'm still walking, but from a different direction. There's supposed to be some paramedics who are going to be expecting me, so if you are still in the parking area, stand by them and I'll meet you there."

"Paramedics, ambulance? Luke, what's happened? Please tell me."

Luke tried to respond, but there was no more reception and the call had abruptly ended. He knew Linda was no doubt in a panic, but there was nothing he could do until he saw her.

16

Linda continued to yell into the phone for a response as the deputy and the other searchers stared confused. Realizing their eyes were on her, she put the phone down trying to wipe the tears of frustration that fell from her eyes.

Deputy Fowler stopped and walked toward her.

"What happened, Mrs. Williams?"

"I don't know."

"Was that your husband?"

"Yes . . . he told me they had caught the guy that took Aidan, but I couldn't make anything else out other than some paramedics are on their way here. The phone went dead after that."

"Well, we aren't too far from the park now, so if you need to try to call him again, that's okay. We can give you a few minutes before walking again."

"No, that's quite all right. These nice people need to get home," she said, looking around. "Let's just keep moving."

"Okay ma'am, just wanted to give you the option."

"I really appreciate that, but it's okay. I apologize for being so loud and emotional. I just kinda panicked when the phone went dead."

"It's perfectly reasonable to feel that way," Deputy Fowler said, sympathetically. He walked back to the front of the crowd and motioned everyone forward.

Linda's mind raced, though the crowd continued to walk in silence. She worried for Luke and her heart ached for Aidan. The emotional pain was excruciating as she prayed that Aidan was still alive. Once she was out of the woods, she intended to thank the deputies and the volunteers. Then, she needed to find Luke. Maybe he would call her back and she'd know more, but every step in silence until then was fraught with a plethora of questions.

"Please, God, please," Linda said quietly as more tears wet her face and her lips trembled in the dark.

***

Luke also continued to walk in silence in another area of the woods as he thought of everything that had transpired in the last couple of hours. He was trying to hurry, but he also had to be mindful of the terrain, having fallen earlier. It was difficult but he was trying to stay on the path he was making as much as possible in order to not waste valuable time or get lost in the process on the way back. He didn't like the idea of Detective Stearns staying behind and looking over Chief Roberts and his son's captor, but every moment he delayed only brought more difficulties. With renewed hope and energy, he continued to push back the branches and climb over anything that would keep him from searching further. It broke his heart that they had not found him yet as well as the issue of the phone disconnecting while talking to Linda. He could only hope that she had heard his last words and would meet him at the ambulance. "Hang on, Aidan," Luke said in the dark, hoping that his son was still alive.

The flashlight had begun to dim even more, and Luke tapped it angrily with his hand. "C'mon," he said aloud. The flashlight flickered and then nothing. Luke suddenly began to panic, having only the light of the moon now to guide him. He knew these woods were fairly safe, but there were still snakes and other animals that roamed about and he wasn't exactly an avid hiker or anything close to it. Truth be known, he hadn't taken Aidan camping in some time, and even then, venturing deep into woods really wasn't his forte. Thankfully, he could make out something flashing through the trees. Within a few minutes of fumbling in the dark toward them, he breathed a sigh of relief. He'd finally made it to the clearing. Running now, he could see the paramedics waiting in the parking area where a string of police cars still sat patiently and people milled about unsure whether to leave or stay. Luke continued to run while scanning for Linda, but he did not see her yet. Perhaps she was already with the medics and simply waiting on him to return.

"Hey . . . over here!" Luke yelled as he neared the ambulance.

A couple deputies looked up, confused and unsure of what he was saying.

"I need help . . . help . . ." Luke said, yelling now at the top of his lungs, undeterred by people's stares.

Some of the medics had now begun to take notice as well and within a few minutes, Luke was surrounded by a flurry of officers and medics all trying to find out what was happening. Luke, who was nearly out of breath by the time they began asking him questions, bent down for a moment as he wiped the sweat from his forehead and cleared his throat.

"Mr. Williams, where is Detective Stearns and Chief Roberts?" an officer said, instantly recognizing him.

"The chief has been stabbed . . . we need to go NOW . . . you should follow me please, before it's too late."

The chief you say, how?" one of the other deputies inquired, as he began reaching for the gun in his holster.

"Please, I don't have time for that right now. He's really bad off. He may be gone before we get there. We have to go now." Luke watched as the paramedics ran back to the ambulance to grab their bags of first-aid supplies.

"You are going to need a stretcher too!" Luke called out. "There's no way we can get him out of there unless we haul him out. Please hurry!" He could feel a wave of exhaustion pouring over him, and he closed his eyes. He felt his knees wobbling a bit as if they were about to buckle underneath him.

"Luke . . . Luke!" a familiar voice yelled from the distance.

He opened his eyes again. "Linda!" he said, relieved to know she was near.

"I was so worried about you," she said, wiping away the tears.

"I figured as much, but I'm okay and there's no time for that now. I still have to go with the medics and lead them back to the chief. Just wait for me okay?"

"Honey, I just found you again. I want to go with you. You know I'm capable."

"I never said you weren't, honey. But just like I told you before . . . you need to just trust me and wait."

"Wait . . . where? I can't go home, Luke. I can't. Please . . . all I can think about is Aidan." Linda's eyes pleaded with him as she spoke.

Luke put his hands around her as the medics surrounded them. "I'm sorry, Linda, I have to go now. I promise I *will* bring back our son. Just go to your mom's with the girls and wait by the phone. I'll call you as soon as I can."

Linda was still trying desperately to hold him as he gently pushed her away and headed back into the woods with two other deputies and a couple of paramedics. Only this time, many more flashlights illuminated the path, making it easier for Luke to quickly guide them back to Stearns, Roy, and the chief. It was if he had renewed energy and purpose. A lot had transpired in the last twelve hours, but it was not all bad. They had his son's captor in custody, and now he would have to lead them to Aidan one way or another. *I'm coming for you, son*, Luke said in his mind as he continued to lead everyone back.

***

Stearns knew the chief was probably dead, but even if he was a grumpy son of a gun, he wasn't going to give up on the old man.

"You're gonna get through this," Stearns said aloud to the incapacitated chief.

Roy looked up and laughed, his mouth caked with dirt. "He can't hear you." His voice raspy and condescending.

Stearns tried to ignore him knowing that people like Roy delighted in dominating and controlling every situation, especially when it was detrimental to others. As anticipated, Roy only grew louder and more defiant as he spat and hurled curse words at the detective and the fallen chief.

Finally, Stearns had just about had enough and growled angrily at Roy to be quiet. But this only served to empower Roy, knowing that he was a proverbial "thorn in the side" of the young detective. He delighted himself with the knowledge that he was annoying and getting under the detective's skin.

"What . . . now I can't speak, Detective?"

"I told you to be quiet, so BE QUIET!" Stearns commanded.

"Or what?" Roy asked defiantly. "You think I'm just shutting up when you got me squirming around on the dirt like a friggin' animal? Well, I don't think so, I know my rights. You can't just do this to me. Besides, if you ever plan on seeing that snot-nosed kid again, you'd better start giving me some respect."

"*You* respect?" Stearns said incredulously. "Forget it. I know what you are and what you're capable of. No way you're getting up off the dirt. Go ahead and continue your antics. But I'm warning you that you're wasting your time."

Roy paused for a moment as if genuinely taking the detective's advice to heart, but after a short period of silence, he began ranting loudly again with the hopes that it would wear Detective Stearns down and make him snap violently, thus giving him some defense to his arrest.

But Stearns was too smart for Roy's deplorable behavior. He was visibly aggravated, but not without control of his own actions. He knew better than to let some creep like Roy get off on his charges because of a simple technicality. Roy was going to stand trial for what he had done and hopefully poor little Aidan Williams had somehow survived. But looking at Chief Roberts dying in a pool of blood, he highly doubted it.

He knew just by observing Mr. Williams that he and his wife continued to believe their son was still alive. He thought about how devastated they would be if Roy led them to his body in exchange for a plea bargain.

Deep down, he knew Roy would do his best to negotiate his jail sentence if he couldn't get under his skin, or worse, manage to sweet talk one of the ignorant parole board members and skedaddle somewhere to avoid accountability for his atrocious acts. *Neither of those scenarios is an option*, Stearns said to himself as he purposely avoided Roy and his snide comments.

"If you're trying to ignore me, it won't work, cop. I got all the time in the world."

Stearns continued to remain stoic and contain his raging emotions. He was hoping that Mr. Williams would be back soon and that, once they booked Roy Brown into the Taylor Police Department, they could begin interrogating him about Aidan and, perhaps, get a confession about Ms. McKenzie's young boy as well.

It was hard to even be near someone so evil and devoid of human reason and decency. He tried to visualize what would have been the case had the time been about a hundred years prior, when no one would have even put him in cuffs; it would have been a noose. "Frontier justice" is waht the old folks had called it.

But times had indeed changed and even people as despicable as Mr. Brown would be entitled to a cell, three square meals, and a fair trial.

Still grimacing at the thought of having to be quiet, Stearns heard a group of voices in the distance and instantly jumped to his feet. A few lights seemed to also appear from nowhere, and he knew immediately that Luke had followed orders and that help was shortly on its way for Chief Roberts. Moving closer toward Roy, who had been lying on the ground for some time now, Stearns offered to allow him to sit up if he promised to keep his mouth shut.

"Why sure," Roy said saucily, though it was nothing more than sugar-coated sarcasm.

"Good," he retorted, pretending to believe him, "'cause we've got company."

"Oh really, who?" Roy said, spitting at the ground.

"Oh no one really . . . just the transportation to your new home, that is, until they sentence you for your crimes."

Roy detected the return of sarcasm in Detective Stearns voice, and it left him seething with anger. *Too bad I have cuffs around my wrists*, he thought. He envisioned making Stearns bleed like the old chief.

The lights became more visible and brighter as the group of medics and officers made their way toward Stearns. Roy watched like a child pleased with his handiwork. The paramedics rushed to attend to the chief and worked feverishly to resuscitate him, but he had already gone into peripheral hypoperfusion due to hypovolemia—in laymen's terms, shock. Both Luke and Stearns were actually surprised that the chief was still alive, but watching how near cardiac collapse he was was almost too much for either. Luke had to look away when one of the medics wiped away more blood that had seeped through the chief's clothing while trying to revive him.

He wasn't unaccustomed to the sight of blood, but this was more than he had ever seen in his life. He instantly felt dizzy and queasy to his stomach. Stearns sensed the change in him and put his hand on Luke's shoulder to steady him.

"You all right, Mr. Williams?"

Luke gulped, a bit embarrassed. "I think so. Maybe I just need to sit down for a minute."

Stearns guided him to another area for him to rest, far enough away from the flurry of commotion. "Better?" Stearns asked, still concerned.

Luke closed his eyes and took a deep breath "Yeah, a bit. Thought I was about to pass out over there. Good thing you steadied me when you did."

"It's only because I've been there. Don't feel bad. Just sit here for a minute while I talk to the other officers about Mr. Brown. Think the medics have the chief on the stretcher, so I think that's a good sign. Perhaps he may just pull through this."

"I don't see how," Luke said, matter-of-factly. "But I hope he does, and that we find my son. I know that every second counts, and I want that creep to tell me where Aidan is. I know he knows, but he wants to keep playing as if it's some kinda sick game. I'm sorry, Detective, but it's taking everything I have not to go over there and put my hands on him and not let go until he tells me what I want to know. I know it ain't right, but I can't help it right now. I'm so frustrated and angry." Luke's fingers were trembling as he spoke.

Stearns did not want Luke to do anything worthy of regret and retaliate against Mr. Brown. Taking a softer approach, Stearns leaned in closer to Luke before speaking. "Mr. Williams . . . Luke . . . , I don't blame you at all for the way you feel, but I also know that we need to do everything by the book or this guy will weasel out of what he has done. Once we get him back to the department, we can begin interrogating him until he confesses and tells us where Aidan is."

Stearns glanced in Roy's direction. He was beaming from ear to ear at all the attention he was getting, but Stearns knew better. Roy was scared even if he didn't want to admit it. "You'd better be," Stearns said quietly to himself as he continued to stare at Roy. There was no way he'd let the judge set bail on this guy.

Luke still felt queasy, but with a couple of the medics and officers were heading back through the woods and toward the ambulance, the wave of nausea began to subside. Now, he and Stearns, along with a medic and another officer, were left with Roy. Luke could feel the hairs on the back of his neck stand up, and his body grew tense as he looked around and waited for him to respond.

Stearns had already bagged the bloody knife as evidence and, letting Roy stand on his feet, proceeded to lead him in cuffs out of the woods along with the remaining party. Luke tried his best to walk as far away from Roy as he could. His fingers still trembled, and he wasn't sure if it was a symptom of anger, fear, or both. Roy had continued to saunter though still in handcuffs, and Luke fought feelings of outrage and desires to confront Roy right then and there. The trek was a good distance and since he had already walked there and back, he was sore and thirsty. His arm still ached, but as he watched Roy appearing sickly apathetic to his recent stabbing of the chief, Luke allowed his swelling anger to fuel him as he pressed on.

Meanwhile, Stearns continued to keep his eyes on Roy, half expecting some hair-brained idea of escape. He watched as Roy tried to quickly ingratiate himself with the other officer who was oblivious to Roy's antics by trying to speak to him.

"I wouldn't do that if I were you," Stearns said rather forcefully.

"What?" Roy said. "Now I can't speak to this officer?"

"No, you can't. You keep your mouth SHUT," Stearns replied. "The only thing that you can say that I want to listen to is the location of the missing boy. So, if you aren't gonna tell us, then keep your mouth shut 'cause we don't care to have you make pleasantries when you just stabbed Chief Roberts to death. You've been read your rights so there's nothing more to say."

Roy didn't like the sound of being bossed around, and as quickly as if a light switch had turned on, his mouth twisted into a maniacal smile. He looked squarely at Detective Stearns and laughed wickedly in defiance. "I'll never tell YOU a thing."

"Oh, you will, soon enough. The game is over, Mr. Brown. In fact, you seem to be the only one who doesn't seem to realize that. So, whatever you think is so gosh-darn funny, well, guess you have finally met a smarter audience than yourself."

"I don't know what you're talking about, Detective. I didn't take any kid, and I resent the way you are speaking to me."

Stearns did not even respond but glanced quickly at Luke. Though he was walking farther behind, Stearns knew that Luke had heard the comments made by Roy and could not afford for him to lose his cool. But Luke simply nodded, understanding that he must remain calm. They both knew that soon Roy would be behind bars and with more pressure

187

to give information, perhaps he would cave in and lead them to Aidan. But while they walked and mused about finding Aidan, Roy grew more and more agitated and angry.

He knew if he was going to negotiate a lesser sentence, he'd have to produce Aidan dead or alive and that was something he couldn't do. *Where can that little sneaky brat be?* he thought. Without knowing, eventually his bargaining chip would disappear, leaving nothing to save his neck from a death sentence. Jail wasn't something he was looking forward to; in fact, if he'd had it his way, both the kid and the old cop would be dead with him long gone and on to another town to lay low for a while until his insatiable desire would return and then . . .

A noise from somewhere in the distance jolted him out of his thoughts, and everyone gasped in astonishment. Stearns pulled his firearm out again and shined the light toward the wooded darkness. Expecting to see an animal, everyone was shocked as Deputy Thompson, a bit disoriented, collapsed before them in a large heap, his mouth trying to form a single word . . . "boy."

Stearns quickly ran toward the deputy with Luke following. Roy, on the other hand, grew more nervous and, moving toward the other officer instead, tried to fade away from the limelight. Perhaps if they were all distracted, he could make a break for it.

17

"What is it, what did you say?" Stearns said, coaxing the tired deputy to speak again.

"The . . . boy . . . I think I found him, but I need some help . . ."

Roy's ears perked up as he listened intently.

"Where?" Luke chimed in. "Can you tell me if my boy's okay?"

Deputy Thompson tried to catch his breath. He'd lost his flashlight climbing down one of the steep hills and while scrambling to try and catch it, he had twisted his ankle. After that, he'd walked blindly toward the commotion in the distance until finally stumbling directly in front of Detective Stearns and the others now also exhausted and weary.

"Do you have any water?" Deputy Thompson asked, trying to still regain his composure.

"No," Stearns said. "Unfortunately, it's all gone, but my guess is that we are no more than ten minutes away from the park, at least if I'm thinking correctly. So, if you can get back on your feet, we can give you a hand and start moving again. Once we get Mr. Roy in custody, you can explain to us where you think the little boy is."

Deputy Thompson looked up and furrowed his eyebrows "Who's Roy?"

Confused, Stearns looked at the deputy and then quickly turned his head to where Roy had been standing moments before. "He's gone!" Stearns said, scanning the area. "He couldn't have gotten too far. Everybody spread out. He's still in cuffs, but he'll do what he can to get away, so DON'T underestimate him. He already took down the

CARRIE SIMON

chief. Do not cut him ANY slack. Now . . . GO!" Luke helped Deputy Thompson get back up on his feet and then ran in the same direction as Detective Stearns. Methodically, Stearns glanced into the darkness. He knew Roy would have been crouching down nearby and a too-hurried look around might allow him to slip through their fingers.

Having Luke a few yards away Stearns signaled as he had previously for Luke to walk slow. Much to their surprise, both of them heard a familiar voice. "Get off me!"

"I got him!" the other deputy exclaimed, much to the chagrin of Roy who had hid behind a large tree about twenty feet away from where he had stood earlier. Sensing a window of opportunity, he had figured the young officer would continue to rant, and he could easily back off undetected. Angrily, he realized the conversation had ended way too soon leaving everyone to look around and thus discovering his intentions of escape. Worse, it was short-lived freedom as he was dragged out from behind the tree and thrust back in the front of the group with no sympathy or regard.

Within minutes of walking in silence, they reached the clearing and Roy finally stood exposed and directly in front of a gathering audience as he exited the woods and saw the flashing lights of the patrol cars. He stared back like a wild beast on display now that he had been captured. Still writhing with anger that his plans had not worked, he spat on anyone close enough to feel his retaliation and hate. Many turned away disgusted, others spat back. Stearns, however, urged the crowd to disperse and leave the officers to do their job. But very few listened. The media had gotten wind of the capture and most simply stood transfixed on the man who had turned the entire town upside down with fear.

Luke had trailed a bit behind this time to speak with Deputy Thompson. He didn't know if the deputy really knew where Aidan was, but he wanted to know more.

"Is my son alive?" Luke asked, offering to allow the deputy to put his arm around Luke's shoulder as he hobbled toward a waiting patrol car.

190

"I don't know. You must be Mr. Williams. I'm so sorry. I really don't know. I didn't see any movement, but I . . ."

"Why didn't you get him?"

"He is in a loft of some sort in an old shed back in the woods." Deputy Thompson pointed back to the woods as he continued to speak.

"How did you see him then? Did you call out his name?" Luke continued to quiz the deputy, wanting to run back into the woods and bring his son to safety.

"I actually didn't see him at first, Mr. Williams. I stumbled upon the old rickety place and by sheer happenstance, I discovered him."

"How's that?" Luke said, unsure of what Deputy Thompson meant.

"Well, it was kinda dark and when I got inside the shed or whatever you wanna call it, I had to hold my nose because it smelled awful. There were broken glass bottles everywhere and some pieces of rope, but I didn't pick them up because I didn't have any gloves."

"Okay, then what?" Luke asked, feasting on every word, as it brought hope of Aidan's whereabouts.

"Well, I was kinda nervous about walking in there without the chief and everything, so I walked a bit further and that's when it fell on me and I looked up."

"What fell on you?"

"Some small drops of blood."

"Oh, dear God." Luke's eyes teared up as he continued to press the deputy for more information. "You say you looked up, what was there?"

"I'll be honest with ya, Mr. Williams, it really scared me 'cause at first I couldn't tell what was up there and whether or not it was big, small, human or not, dead or alive. I kinda jumped back 'cause I realized that . . ." The deputy paused as he winced in pain.

"Realized what?" Luke bellowed while wringing his hands.

"That the place was too small for a grown man and that I really needed more help. I was scared to radio anyone because we were told to refrain from as much noise as possible with the kidnapper still on the loose and hiding out. I thought I heard yelling after I had injured my ankle, but there wasn't anything I could do. I'm guessing that was the chief, but I just kept hobbling in this direction, hoping that I'd run into somebody besides the kidnapper and get some help."

"But you really think it was my son?"

"I think it might be, but I didn't see any movement, even when I shined the light. I wish I could help, but I don't know anything more and I wouldn't make it back there with my ankle the way it is now."

"No, you've helped more than enough. I am going to go check it out myself," Luke said as he walked away and toward Detective Stearns.

Luke wanted to call Linda back and tell her what the deputy had told him, but the more he thought about it as he approached Stearns the more he realized that it was better to just wait and see if it really was Aidan and if he was still alive. His heart sank as he listened to the deputy tell him the news he dreaded . . . drops of blood . . . no movement.

"Detective, now that Roy's in custody . . . we gotta go back and get my son."

Stearns looked up from the conversation with the other law officers as Roy was being placed into one of the patrol cars and driven off.

"What was that?" Stearns said.

Luke repeated himself. "We got to go back, PLEASE. Deputy Thompson found Aidan . . . or at least he thinks he did. You remember that shed we saw while we were walking? Well, I think that's the one the deputy is talking about."

"Whoa, you're talking a mile a minute, Mr. Williams. Tell me exactly what the deputy told you."

Luke tried to relax and relate the conversation as quickly but as accurately as he could, trying to remember to pause in between sentences. Stearns took in every word, but his face did not denote one way or another as to how he felt.

Finally, Luke finished and furrowed his eyebrows, somewhat disappointed in the silence that followed, still hoping that Detective Stearns was still as passionate about finding Aidan as he was.

"Well, what are we waiting for?" Stearns said, grasping his flashlight and signaling for one of the medics to accompany them back in the woods.

Luke eagerly grabbed a flashlight, as well as his cell phone, and followed. He thought again about speaking with Linda, but he decided it was best to leave her alone for now.

Within minutes, they were back traipsing through the woods with Stearns leading them to the area where he had seen the shed. He surmised that the footprints he had discovered earlier were probably Deputy Thompson's. Thankfully, even in darkness the deputy had managed to hobble his way directly in front of them instead of dangling a few feet high in one of the traps that he and Luke had uncovered earlier.

No doubt there would be more—not necessarily fashioned in the same way—so while Stearns wanted to run to get to their destination faster, but he had to be cautious. If Aidan had been killed already, it didn't make much sense to also endanger everyone else's life, knowing full well it might be the next morning before help might be able to reach them. As he suspected, Luke pushed forward with the fervent fever of a father in pursuit of his son. But Stearns knew he would have to make him understand that he could not just run all over creation without regard for his own self. The woods had a multitude of dangers regardless of any intentional snares.

The medic who had also agreed to go with them, on the other hand, looked more nervous than anything. He was younger than Stearns and obviously fresh out of training. Getting a call about someone having chest pains and heading to the local hospital was one thing, but Stearns knew this was something completely different and well out of the realm of experience for this novice.

"You doing okay over there?" Stearns asked as he watched the medic struggle to keep up. Thanks to Mr. Williams' desire to find his son, little had been needed in the form of motivation. If anything, he was telling Mr. Williams to slow down and the young medic to pick up the pace.

"I'm all right," he replied, trying to push another small tree branch away from his face with little success. Stearns tried to help, but by doing so it only made matters worse as both tried to walk in unison.

"It's fine, really," the medic said after, visibly agitated.

Stearns took the hint and moved a few feet away, but still kept his eye out in the event he was needed.

"It can't be much further," Luke called out after another hour of hiking up the terrain.

"I sure hope not," Stearns said. He made sure no one was lagging too far behind. "My legs are killing me. And here I am thinking I'm in shape."

Luke had his own aches, as well. His feet were tired and his forearm hurt from the long gash, but pain seemed to not be a hindrance as the drudgery of heading back into the woods became a necessity to finding Aidan. It was almost as if he could not reach him fast enough. Hopefully, the deputy was correct. Luke dreaded the possibility of finding his son dead, and he didn't know how he would tell Linda if that was the outcome. No parent should have to make funeral arrangements for his own child. "Please God. If he's there, let him be alive. Even if it's just barely . . . please." Luke mouthed the words silently as he waited a couple of seconds for Stearns to decide which way to turn. Most of the area looked vaguely familiar but knowing that Stearns probably was aware of the best direction to take, he deferred to him and waited.

Stearns knew that Luke had waited for his lead and, taking a brief moment to look out across the distance, he pointed toward an area more closely wooded than the rest. "I think we need to go this way," Stearns said. He shined the flashlight over his head to get both Luke's and the medic's attention.

"Are you sure?" Luke asked incredulously.

"I believe so. Of course we aren't in the exact spot as when we originally saw the shed in the distance, but this area does look familiar to me even though we're coming from a different direction. Besides, I know if we continue to travel this way, even if we're fifty to hundred yards away, we can still shine the light out to guide us the rest of the way there. Not likely that we run exactly right into it. So, let's head that way and just keep our eyes and ears open."

"Agreed," Luke said. He and the young medic nodded in unison.

The moon was now shining directly over them, and the unseen animals had begun to make an array of strange noises, from chirping to quick, fleeting movements through the trees and foliage. The melody of their sounds was eerie and unsettling, but everyone walked quickly in silence as each man remained determined to not stumble or lag behind.

Stearns continued to shine his flashlight in the direction they were heading and also on the ground below, being cognizant that there was also a variety of venomous snakes that were indigenous to the area.

"Make sure you watch where you step too," Stearns yelled out as they continued to plod toward their goal.

Finally, Luke spotted the old caved-in shed and waved his flashlight at Stearns and the medic. "Look . . . there it is," Luke said, almost losing his footing.

"Okay, good job but before we go rushing over there, let's not forget the traps that almost got us earlier.

"Traps?" the naïve medic asked, looking confused. "I thought you got the guy that did this, right?"

"Yeah, we did, but he's a crafty one and he made some rudimentary traps that Mr. Williams and I would have landed in had we not been careful where we walked. No telling what else he's got around here. Let's get going but nobody run ahead without looking."

Stearns walked slowly but decisively toward the shed. The smell was so pungent that they all shuddered at the entrance of the old and rickety structure, cringing as they stepped back in order to get a deep breath of clean air. The smell of feces was overpowering, and even Luke put his shirt over his face to avoid the wave of nausea as he thought of all the horrible things that may have transpired since Aidan had been kidnapped.

"We are going to have to go in but be careful. No telling what we will find. I remind you not to touch anything, as everything is considered evidence." Stearns slowly moved in past the entrance, shining the flashlight on the floor and grimacing as the light revealed the decay and filth of the floor. Grotesquely arrayed with glass and overgrown ivy, the building itself was appalling. Dark areas that Stearns wasn't sure whether it was excrement or something else also left a mental impression that only secrets of horror existed within what was left of such a place. Some of the other areas also looked as if, even in its deplorable state, it had been ransacked. Stearns could only imagine what had taken place to warrant such behavior. Each one of them stepped slowly around, afraid to touch anything even with their feet.

"The deputy told me he saw something up top, said it dripped blood on him," Luke said.

Stearns shined his light up at the roof where pieces of wood jaunted angrily out of place, and long tendrils of ivy and other plants had forged through making it somewhat difficult to see what had caved in and what was really at the top of the shed.

"It's difficult to see up there, but it doesn't look like anything other than rotted wood and vines. Am I missing something?"

Luke wasn't sure. "Maybe we check a little further toward the back of this place. I got the impression it was like a loft of some sort. He said it was too small for anything big, so my guess is Aidan might've crawled up there and hid."

"Maybe," Stearns said, "or got stuffed up there. You said the deputy told you there was blood."

Luke cringed. He didn't want to think that way or be forced to think that way, at least not now. "Let's keep looking. One way or another, I'm not giving up until I find him and bring him home."

Stearns continued to slowly lead them further as he shined the light above, looking for anything that might be what Mr. Williams was describing.

The medic was obviously skittish, but simply followed, no doubt unsure what to contribute to the conversation.

"Be looking for something on the walls," Stearns said as he turned to face Luke.

"Why is that?"

"'Cause if he did get up there by himself, then he had to have climbed up somehow, right?"

"Yeah, that makes sense," Luke said quickly, moving away and beginning to scan the perimeter for something to climb up on. Some of the wood slats had a type of fungus growing over them, and others had rusty nails protruding from what was left of them, so Luke tried to just shine the beam of light toward the general area instead of touching the walls with his hands. It didn't appear that anything was worthy of extra attention, but as he moved further about, he noticed an area completely covered in thick ivy tendrils and near what appeared to be the back of the shed. At first glance, he wanted to just peruse over it and move toward other areas, but something nagged at him as if he were missing something. He moved closer to get a better look. *Can't hurt right? Leave no stone unturned*, he thought. Carefully brushing back some of the ivy, something slightly darker behind them and barely visible caught his eye.

"Hey!" Luke called out. "There is something here!"

Stearns and the medic quickly walked over to Luke and brushed back the long and flowery green tendrils, revealing small wooden boards just enough to use the tip of a foot to climb up on. Not really large enough for the average adult, but certainly plausible for a kid.

"Think you can see where this leads?" Luke asked.

"That's what I'm trying to do," Stearns said, using his flashlight to shine up the wall and over more ivy that appeared to accumulate in a large pile directly overhead. "Help me get this ivy out of the way so we can get a better look."

The medic put down the items he had brought with him, and both he and Luke grabbed a handful to pull it down. The tendrils were taut and as each of them were tugged downward, it seemed as if more continued to reappear. But with every effort, new encouragement arose in their hearts as the idea of finding Aidan became not just a hope but a reality.

"Aidan . . . Aidan . . . you up there?" Luke called out, his voice choking despite the cries. "It's Daddy. I'm here, son. Can you hear me?"

Silence was the only response as Luke continued to call out. With more and more ivy beginning to give way, Stearns decided to quit pulling and shined the flashlight at the area that now, despite a few remaining spots, lay almost bare from all their effort.

He gasped loudly, and both Luke and the medic looked up to where the flashlight was shining. At last, they had found what they were looking for. There, jutting out ever so slightly, was a small loft with only a few unbroken slats holding the bottom together and a dark object lying inside of it.

"Oh dear God. No!" Luke said as they hoisted him up enough to touch the bottom.

"Well?" Stearns stated. Luke tried to push his fingers through the planks to feel what was there before responding.

"It's Aidan. I know it. We gotta find a way to get him outta there."

"Is he responsive? Did you feel a heartbeat?" the medic asked, opening up the large bag he'd brought with him.

"No, I can't even tell if he's breathing. Whatever I felt was wet. Maybe we can pull these slats down and catch him."

"I can barely hold you up," Stearns said curtly.

"Please try," Luke pleaded.

"Okay, see if you can pull them down or at least a couple of them, so we can maybe squeeze him outta there."

Luke mustered as much strength as he possibly could. He could hear the wood creaking and groaning as he pulled down hard against the nails with his weight. The effort was just enough to bring a couple of the slats down and Luke tumbling over on top of Stearns. "Whoa!" he said as he looked up from the ground to see a small, bloody hand dangling from the loft.

"Get him down quick!" Stearns said as they all stood back up.

18

Detective Stearns, Luke, and the medic frantically ran through the woods with Luke holding the bloody and unconscious body of his only son. Despite the tattered and reeking clothes, Luke held him tightly, desperately praying for his recovery and thanking God for his answered prayer. The terrain was a struggle, but now that they had Aidan, each man fought against time and statistics to secure the injured boy into the hands of competent physicians.

"How's he doing?" Stearns asked as they slowed down to cross over some of the rougher terrain.

"I'm not sure. I just know he's breathing, and that's all I care about right now," Luke replied.

"We don't have much more to go. I'll phone the hospital to let them know we will be headed there soon."

"Normally, paramedics do that in route," the young medic replied, trying to be helpful.

"Okay," Stearns said gratefully, "just as long as one of us makes sure everything is ready with no delays."

The medic nodded and they all continued in stride toward the clearing. Using his own phone to call dispatch to send an ambulance back to the previous location, he frowned when he couldn't get any service.

"No worries," Stearns said as they got closer and closer to the park. "Keep trying. We are still in an area with very little reception."

Finally, after reaching the clearing, the medic announced aloud that one was on its way.

"Good," Stearns said. "You know, we can go in my truck; it may be faster." Stearns pointed to where he had parked hours before.

"You think there's room for all of us?" Luke inquired, clinging tighter to Aidan.

"I think so. I know the ambulance is coming, but we're losing valuable time here. Let's go now, if you're agreeable to just having me drive."

"Heck yeah. What are we waiting for?" Luke said emphatically, staring at the medic and Detective Stearns. With everyone in the truck, Stearns raced down the long road back to Taylor while the medic called the hospital to let them know they were on the way and indicated they would no longer need the ambulance.

Luke, who sat nearest to the window, held Aidan still as best as he could. Though Stearns was speeding to the hospital, to Luke it seemed like an eternity before they finally arrived and burst through the doors of the ER.

"Get a doctor here fast!" Stearns said, politely barking orders.

Some of the nurses instantly recognized Aidan from the local news station and quickly brought a bed to wheel him back to the physicians on duty at the time. Luke quickly dialed Linda.

"Sir, you have to make calls outside," one of the nurses insisted.

Luke did not want to leave Aidan, but he knew Linda needed to be with him. "Okay, okay," he said, waving his hand in the air and feeling frustrated. Quickly running outside, he dialed her number again. As he waited for her to pick up, he nodded to Stearns who was headed to the police station to interrogate Roy. "Linda?"

"Yes, Luke. It's me. What happened? Why are you so out of breath?"

"We found Aidan, honey. He's alive!"

Linda began sobbing uncontrollably, overwhelmed by her emotions but still trying to speak. "Where is he, Luke? Let me talk to him, please."

"I can't, Linda."

"Why?" she asked loudly.

"Because he's unconscious."

"What? How? I mean, why is he unconscious? What happened to our boy, Luke?"

Luke could hear panic in Linda's voice. "Honey, he has lost some blood and might have gone into shock or something. That's as best as I can describe it without hearing from the doctor."

"Doctor? Does that mean you are at a hospital? Which one? I'm coming there right now." Linda was a bundle of nerves and talking ninety miles a minute.

"Slow down," Luke interjected.

Linda got quiet, realizing that she was ranting.

"Now," Luke said calmly, "we are at Taylor General. He hasn't been seen by a doctor yet, but since I had to step out to call you, he may be on his way now. If the girls are okay, then please come. I'll wait for you."

"The girls are sleeping. I'm on my way. I love you."

Luke walked back into the emergency room after telling Linda good-bye. He knew she was feeling overwhelmed, but once there he would be able to console her as they waited patiently for further news of Aidan's condition.

Spying the nurse that had told him earlier to walk outside, he inquired about Aidan. Sensing the duress in his voice, she informed him that they had already taken Aidan back and that Dr. Johnston would be the attending physician.

"Am I able to go back there?" Luke asked. He wanted desperately to hold his son's hand and comfort him in some way.

"I'm afraid not, but the doctor should be out here shortly and you can talk to him then."

Luke's heart sank but he knew that this was another moment out of his control and best left to prayer. Thanking the nurse before she walked away, he sat down on a large, oversized chair and waited for Linda to arrive. Though his body was exhausted, his mind raced as he wondered how Detective Stearns was doing sitting face-to face with the maniac who had taken Aidan.

Don't think about it, Luke said to himself. He felt the anger swelling inside of him. Justice would be served and he needed to quit thinking about that and focus on what was more important—Aidan's life. Bowing his head he called out again to God, this time so engrossed in prayer that he didn't even see Linda run through the emergency room doors.

"Luke . . . Luke . . .?" Linda said, poking his shoulder once she had noticed him sitting in the waiting area. "Are you sleeping?"

"No. Just trying to sit here with my eyes shut for a moment because I am completely worn out."

Linda put her arms around him as she sat down and patiently waited to hear more about Aidan. As they held each other's hand, Luke recited everything that had happened since they had parted ways in the woods. It was an emotional conversation for both. Each struggled to make sense of everything and be grateful despite such an ordeal. Linda didn't understand why they couldn't see Aidan, but she knew if God had seen them through it all thus far, then she simply needed to trust Him and be obedient.

The minutes soon turned to hours, and Luke and Linda patiently waited. Finally, a large door opened and a middle-aged man with gray, tousled hair and dressed in a white lab coat walked toward them and extended his hand. Luke took it in his and shook it firmly.

"Mr. and Mrs. Williams, I presume?"

"Yes . . ."

"My name is Doctor Johnston."

"Doc, how is he doing?"

"That's exactly why I'm here, to talk to you about your son."

"Oh, Doctor . . . please tell us that he is okay," Linda said, her voice stricken with worry.

"I suspect he will be just fine physically with time, though mentally, that is beyond my realm of expertise. Though, my opinion is that had he remained in the state he was found for another twelve to twenty-four hours, I do not believe your son would be with us today. He is still suffering from shock, but we have already stitched up his wounds and put him in a private room so that you can be with him from now on. I'm sure with time, therapy, and extensive counseling he should make a full recovery."

"Don't forget prayer, Doc," Luke replied to the physician's comments.

"Ah, yes . . . prayer. Everyone needs that," he said with a reassuring smile.

"Thank you for taking care of our son," Linda called out as Dr. Johnston was paged to attend to someone else.

"It was my pleasure. I'll make my rounds in the morning to see how he's doing." Dr. Johnston walked briskly back though the door and out of sight. Both Luke and Linda stared at each other. Finally, they would be able to see Aidan, hold his hand, and whisper "I love you" even if he couldn't hear them.

A petite nurse stepped into the waiting room a few moments later and scanned the few people who were sitting there. "Are you the Williamses?" she called out.

"Yes," Linda said quickly before Luke could interject.

"All right, please follow me."

She held a chart in one hand and used the other to usher Luke and Linda through the large door that Dr. Johnston had recently entered and down the long corridor to Aidan's room.

"All right, here we are," she said slowly, hanging the chart on the side of the door. "You both can go on in. Your son is recuperating right now from the minor operation and is probably still sedated. So, if you need anything, just ring for me and I'll be here shortly."

Luke and Linda thanked her and stepped inside. The room wasn't very large but a small loveseat and chair sat to the side of the bed, giving a comfortable place to sit near Aidan where he lay still and motionless.

He looked sad as if his dreams were unpleasant, and Linda immediately put his cover closer around his thin body and stroked his hair. Luke sat down on the chair and watched, aghast at Aidan's appearance.

It was Aidan all right, but almost unrecognizable. His small frame looked even more fragile, and his face appeared disfigured, discolored, and scratched. Even his eyelids looked swollen, and the marks around his wrists were painfully visible. Luke winced, trying hard to hold back tears. Searching for Aidan had been difficult enough, but looking at what he had endured was almost unbearable.

"Oh, Luke," Linda said. She ran her fingers over the marks on his face and wrists.

"I know, baby. It's gonna be an uphill battle for a while, but God answered our prayers and our son is with us. Can you imagine those parents who never find their child or like Ms. McKenzie . . . too late?"

"I can't, Luke. The pain must be devastating. I can see now why Ms. McKenzie is the way she is. Poor woman, I hope she has some closure now that her son's killer is behind bars," Linda replied, a chill running down her spine, knowing at some point, they would have to face him, but for now, only Aidan's recovery mattered, no matter how long that would take. As he slept, now in the hands of those who loved him, Luke and Linda waited with anticipation for Aidan to open his eyes and be rejoined with them.

A month later the phone rang, and as Luke put the phone to his ear, a familiar voice spoke loudly.

"Mr. Williams, this is Detective Stearns. Just calling to check on your son."

Luke smiled to himself, admiring the detective's concern, "Well, frankly he is improving far better than we could have imagined. Had you asked me a month ago while he was lying in a hospital bed, I'd have told you something different. But he's really healing up nicely, and with counseling, he's starting to open up about what happened to him and begin to play and laugh like he used to. We don't expect everything to be the way it was before, at least not for a long time and maybe not ever, but we know we have witnessed a miracle with his return and we can't do anything but be grateful."

"I thought as much," Stearns said. "I meant to say something when I saw you and your wife at Chief Roberts' funeral, but it just didn't seem right at the time, and I knew that you and your family had quite a lot to cope with already."

"Well, we did and still do. But we wouldn't have minded, Detective. You helped us save our boy, and for that we are eternally in your debt. We just couldn't miss the chief's funeral, even in the midst of our own problems. He wasn't the easiest person to be around, but he risked his life to find Aidan and he ultimately died because of it." Luke pulled the phone away from his face as he cleared his throat and wiped the tears beginning to form in his eyes.

"Mr. Williams? You all right? I didn't mean to upset you by calling."

"Oh, I'm fine, just so humbled by everyone's sacrifice. How about yourself? The news for the last week hasn't been too eventful, which I'm sure you're glad about since the first couple of weeks had you basically on every news station."

"Ughh, it was more nerve-racking than anything to be honest with you," Stearns said, letting out a long sigh. "Once the media found out we had Roy in custody, it was a melee. I couldn't even go home for at least a week without a microphone being shoved in my face."

"They tried to get us to comment and give our side of the story, but we politely declined," Luke said sympathetically.

"Well, enjoy it for now because when the trial starts, they'll be back."

"What do you mean?" Luke asked, trying to get a better understanding of what was in the horizon.

"We, that is, the DA's office and myself, are preparing to pursue the death penalty, and once we go to court the media will be in full force, and you and Mrs. Williams will no doubt be thrust into the limelight with your presence there. So, I strongly suggest that you both prepare yourselves for the onslaught of questions and those who want to just make the five o'clock news. When it happens, and I assure you it will, you and your wife will need to make arrangements to probably shield your children from the frenzy, especially Aidan."

"We will, Detective. Trust me, we have come this far, and we don't want any setbacks for Aidan or our family."

"I don't want that either, Mr. Williams. I'll keep you informed. I've already notified Ms. McKenzie, so that she can also be prepared."

"How is she coping?" Luke asked.

"I think she also has a long road ahead, but now that there is a face and a name to the killer of her son, she feels assured that he will stand and answer for the atrocities he has done. I believe in my heart that it gives her some comfort in knowing that he has now been caught and that her attempts at trying to find out who took her son and why are over. I hope she can heal now and move on with her life."

"I hope so too," Luke said. He remembered how sad and distraught Ms. McKenzie had sounded. Perhaps they could invite her to church.

"Well, I won't keep you any longer," Stearns said after another couple of minutes.

"I'm really glad you called, Detective. I mean you're practically like family now. If there is anything we can do for you, just say the word."

Stearns chuckled. "I'm just fine. The only thing I want is for y'all to be okay and this town to be safe."

"Well, with a detective like you, I'm sure we are gonna be in good hands."

"Now, you're just trying to butter me up," Stearns said. "Let's just say I'll do my best and leave it at that."

"Fair enough. Did you think about what I asked you last time?"

"Uh, church? I dunno, Mr. Williams, I guess I'm still thinking about it."

"All right, no pressure. But if you want to, it starts at eleven in the morning, and you are welcome to come and sit with us."

Stearns hung up the phone, still debating about whether or not he wanted to go as Mr. Williams had suggested or make other plans. He had been so busy lately that he hadn't even conversed with Sarah as usual or made silly excuses to bring something for her to analyze at the lab. *Maybe she might go with me tomorrow*, he thought as he tried to get up the courage to call her. *Oh, but I'm sure she's probably busy with a million different things to do*, the voice of procrastination uttered. But this time Stearns ignored it and quickly dialed her number before he lost his nerve.

"Sarah, it's me . . . Maris. You got a minute?"

"Sure thing, what's going on, something wrong?"

"No, just thought I'd call you . . . I mean, if that's okay."

"Sure, why wouldn't it be?" Sarah asked pleasantly, a bit surprised at the unexpected phone call.

"Well, you might be busy or something," Stearns replied, still fumbling with how to ask her out.

"Nope, I kinda keep an open calendar when I'm not at work. You?"

"Oh, not doing too much myself either. But well . . . see . . . the Williamses have asked me or rather invited me to their church tomorrow morning, and I . . . wanted to see if you might care to join me." Stearns waited as a long pause ensued.

"Hmm, don't think I've ever had a guy just outta the blue invite me to church," Sarah said giggling.

Stearns suddenly felt his face feel warm, and he was grateful that Sarah was not there to witness it. He felt silly now that he had asked so blatant a question and wondered if he should simply hang up and tell her the next time at work that it had been a bad connection.

He tried to laugh it off, joining in her obvious fit of giggles. "Yeah, well no big deal . . . I'll just see you on Monday."

"Wait," Sarah said, suddenly becoming serious. "I just said no one had ever asked me that, but I didn't say I wouldn't go. Just tell me what time I would need to meet you and then maybe we could grab some coffee or something . . . nothing fancy."

Stearns couldn't believe his ears. The phone almost dropped out of his hands with anticipation. "Okay . . . um, you know that church on the corner of Monroe and Minden? Well, it's right there, and Mr. Williams told me that it starts at 11:00 a.m. I'm assuming it should take about an hour or so. Afterward, if you want coffee, that's fine, or if you want lunch, we can do that too." Stearns felt elated at the prospect of taking Sarah out on a date.

"Sounds good," Sarah said, and hung up the phone.

The following day, Stearns dressed in his nicest suit, drove over to the church, and sat down in one of the pews. He was a bit early, but that was far better than being late. And he was nervous thinking of Sarah and whether or not she would show up as promised. Linda was the first to spot him when she entered into the sanctuary from her Sunday school class with Luke, Aidan, and their two girls following closely behind. Her eyes lit up as she motioned to Luke that he had been able to make it.

"Oh, Mr. Stearns," Aidan said, running toward him with his arms open, seemingly undeterred by Linda's comments to just walk. "Thank you so much for listening."

"Listening?" Stearns asked, somewhat puzzled. He studied Aidan's face, still noticeably scarred in some areas.

"Yes, I kept asking God to send help and He sent you and my dad to find me; I knew He would."

Aidan quickly wrapped his arms around Detective Stearns and embraced him. The heartfelt gesture caught Stearns completely off guard and a lump welled up in his throat as he hugged him fiercely back. Now, fully understanding the magnitude of his responsibility, he vowed to always pursue justice for all those missing and remain hopeful for their safe return.

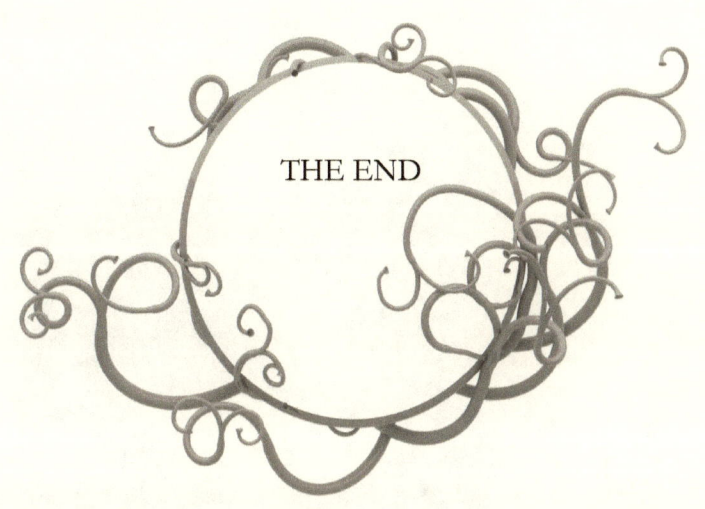

THE END

www.ingramcontent.com/pod-product-compliance
Lightning Source LLC
Chambersburg PA
CBHW020557250626
47154CB00004B/1257